dying for veronica

3. "Some day I'll be a Sister like you, and teach!"

dying for veronica

a sub-catholic dream with mind-music

a novel by matthew d remski

INSOMNIAC PRESS

Edited by Mike O'Connor
Copy edited by Lloyd Davis & Liz Thorpe
Designed by Mike O'Connor

Canadian Cataloguing in Publication Data

Remski, Matthew, 1971-
      Dying for Veronica

ISBN 1-895837-40-5

I. Title.

PS8585.E47D9   1997   C813'.54   C96-932448-0
PR9199.3.R45D9   1997

Printed and bound in Canada

Insomniac Press
378 Delaware Ave.
Toronto, Ontario, Canada, M6H 2T8

Insomniac Press acknowledges the support received for its publishing program from the Canada Council's Project Grant Program.

this book is for dennison smith

The author would like to gratefully acknowlege the following persons and events for support, encouragement and grace. Marianne Armstrong, John Barlow, Stan Bevington, Christian Bök, Tony Burgess, Paul Butler, Lynn Crosbie, Saro d'Agostino, Christopher Dewdney, Father Pier Giorgio Di Cicco, The Future Bakery, Steven Heighton, Mark Hickmott, Michael Holmes, Luciano Iacobelli, Bill Kennedy, Mary Lindsay, Peter McPhee, Steve McCaffery, Karen MacCormack, Oceana, David Jill and Andrew Remski, Stan Rogal, Richard Stipl, Michelle Teran and the Sternberk Augustinian Monastery Installation Symposium, Richard M. Vaughan, Darren Wershler-Henry and Eddy Yanofsky. Thanks to Ian Wilson for helping to find the cover photograph.

The book exists in its present form due to the editorial guidance and spiritual inspiration of Dennison Smith.

Excerpts have appeared under various titles in Quarry Magazine, The New Quarterly, Oversion: The Postraphaelite Magazine of Free Writing and Correspondence, and Pan del Muerto.

I also thank the Ontario Arts Council and the Roman Catholic Church for all that rent money.

"...a certain devil was found to bee the autor of all this ill, bewraying himself by voice, and unaccustomed words and sentences, as well Latin as Greek (though the patient were ignorant of the Greek tongue): he laied open manie secrets of the by-standers, and chiefly of the Physicians, derideing them for that they had abused all mannere of medicament to the patient's great harm, and becaus they had brought his bodie so low by needless purgations."

Ambroise Paré (from a tract on epilepsy, 1649)

Perhaps death is always incestuous — a fact that would only add to its spell. The "soul sister" is its spiritualized version. The great stories of seduction, that of Phaedra or Isolde, are stories of incest, and always end in death. What are we to conclude, if not that death itself awaits us in the age-old temptation of incest, including in the incestuous relation we maintain with our own image? We are seduced by the latter because it consoles us with the imminent death of our sacrilegious existence.

Jean Baudrillard, *Seduction*

Before you write about creatures which can fly, make a book about insensible things which descend in the air without the wind, and another about those which descend with the wind.

Da Vinci, *On Flight**

* Irma A. Richter provides the translation here, not only from the Italian, but also from its original right-to-left disposition, for Da Vinci was a mirrorist: he wrote backwards. Would that my publisher had let me write backwards, thus reversing the textual conveyor belt that has pulled me to my narrative death. Then I

might have been the bird that returns first to nest and then to egg, all after waking up and stretching the rigour out of its wings at the foot of a shiny bank tower, in whose mirrors it became seduced by the image of itself, and so crashed and died. If such backwards-writing had been practicable (read: marketable), my gentle publisher would have included a mirror in the dustjacket sleeve. Then you, Veronica, my sweet sister, could read this letter to you in reflection, and I would lie in my grave imagining that some obsequious tremor of your hand might totter the glass away from the page, and you would be startled by the image of your own beautiful eyes.

Typographical Legend:

This is the font of conventional narration, to which the author turns first to move Events along: chronologically concerned, interested in descriptive documentation, accented with confident self-reflexivity, educated in an environment of sophisticated epistemological methods. (But beware of Capitalization, parentheses, oversized commas, and all other conspicuous acts of **EMPHASIS**,)

This is the font of dreams and certain iconic figures, what the author tries to resist because of an innate distaste for generic Victoriana: Other, highly theatrical, unbelievable yet imperative, a disruptive genophone creating the vacuum into which it is pulled, such memory in apostrophic flight, such psalms that linger like seedless first fruit.

This is the font of outdated technology (c. 1910 - 1968): unitary, serialized, generating syntactic nostalgia among the ontologically unstable. How monasteries speak with the Grammar of Catholic Fatigue. That which the author wants to believe as much as it believes itself, so as to be able to reconstruct Home out of spilled candlewax and dust on confessional floors.

This is the font of unreflexive onto-confidence, id est, the Nineteenth Century. Employed by popes and prayerbooks. Unfortunately, this lettering is not illuminated in our present time with those pretty strokes of red and gold.

this is the font of poorly simulated handwriting, employed to suggest spontaneity when the author is hypersensitive to the mediations of print. used for those words that are so immediate and present that they seem to be written over the shoulder of the reader, into spaces left by an inde-cisive author. also may suggest impromptu markings by subsequent readers.

This is the post-font of computer commands, employed to suggest cool post-accuracy and post-objectivity, a post-ruse that collapses when it is used to print the post-words "simula-tion", "relativity", and "decon-struction".

THIS IS THE FONT OF METANOIC SCHIZOPHRE-NIA, WHAT THE AUTHOR SEEMS TO EXCRETE SPASMODICALLY: WANDERING IN THE ALIEN-ATION BETWEEN INVERTED COMMAS, UNABLE TO DISTINGUISH WHAT IT READS (HEARS) FROM WHAT IT WANTS TO WRITE (SCREAM).

✴❈❉▲ ❉▲ ▼❈❅ ❆❏■▼ ❏❆ ❆❏❒❍▲ ❐❒❅✍
▲❅❒❖❅❄ ❏■●❙ ❉■ ❆❏▲▲❉●✎ ✴❈❏◆❇❈
❉●●❅❇❉❂●❅ ▼❏ ❍❏▲▼✌ ❉▼ ❉▲ ▼❈❅ ❍❏▲▼
❈❏■❅▲▼ ❆❏■▼ ❁❖❁❉●❁❂●❅ ▼❏ ▼❈❏▲❅
❅❘❈❁◆▲▼❅❄ ◗❉▼❈ ▼❈❅❏●❏❇❙✌ ❐▲❙❃❈❏●❏❇❙✌
■❁❒❒❁▼❏●❏❇❙✌ ▲❅❍❁■▼❉❃▲ ❁■❄ ❁●●
❆❏❒❍▲ ❏❆ ❐▲❅◆❄❏✍■❁▼◆❒❁●✍❒❅❁●❉▲❍✎

This is the font of Veronica, the true image, my sister, my teacher, my lover — to whom this book is both singed mass card and black velvet memorial.

1.

i crave redemptive dreams, i warn you all. everywhere there are purple stains in the snow. (and all sleep is bitter, no matter who lies down beside you, whether gentle sister or terrorist)

2.

Veronica, you used to wake me up by sitting on my face. You straddled my head and hissed

wake up. wake up little one and smell me. go on smell me. smell it. go on little boy, smell me.

(wriggle wriggle squirm ... sniff sniff)

good. now. good morning to you.

Her thighs flattened my ears. Her voice muffled by a History of Polyfilla, Oblivion Duvets. (The room filled with the light you see when the purple curtains of your confessional cleave open like the dress of a whore mounting the steps of a gallows.)

3.

...wet condom on my orange-crate night table like wasted skin-graft... ultrasound glow of my St. Francis reading lamp... there's a rosary with turquoise plastic beads... disco-facetted... i'm twenty-three, waking up alone again in toronto with no idea who was here or not here last night (perhaps I was alone — but then, why the condom? — "...for we must all protect ourselves from the bilious alluvia of selfhood" as St. Anselm says...) and there hasn't been a letter from my sister for weeks and she's nowhere near a phone   i'm writing to you, Veronica... i've lined up the polaroids in the silverblue morning... i remember the teaching: *begin by praying.* I am obedient by nature.

Hear please the begging in my voice like a pigeon scratching the wet plaster by which she has been sealed. There was rain today and then there was not. There was a man sleeping beneath my window and then a boy squatted beside him and then stood up and ran back to the stoop from which he had emerged and the man woke up and stretched and wandered away. There was a sister in my dream dreamt here at my desk but that ended too.

O God allow me to eavesdrop on those who sing alone in bare rooms. Let my solitary games be ruled by the improvisation of those children in the street. Let my body be charged with the endings of tiny things. Let my mind wander over the preparation of simple food. Let me pause over the perfections of apples on the fruit stand and construct an arbitrary criterion for choosing one for my body to eat. Let me fast because it has become enough to simply LOOK at Matter. Let my breathing be of a single garment with tidal factors in this landlocked city of Toronto. Let my spine be a happily planted compass point for the hysterical arcs of my praise, now slower, now breathless. My cup with sludge of red wine. This arrangement of things is dressing me for eternity.

Soon it will be recess time in the schoolyard below and the ugly boys and girls will be excluded from games and tormented with words and I pray for them now in advance. Soon the man who has replaced my father as the cathedral bellringer will climb into the tower to ring out the Angelus over carhorn and muffled urban convulsion. Samaritans will get mugged today. Am I comforted by universal constants?

When it rained the beads of water ran down the slanting telephone wires like indicators on radio dials tuned by a hand that hears nothing of interest.

4.

BE HAPPY IF THE WORLD DESPISES YOU. Veronica!
What will the numbers say on your headstone against
which I will lean these papers — letterhead of insomnia,
blotter for wino piss? What do any numbers say? Where
are you? Are you in the kitchen with our cathedral-maid
mother, kneading unleavened host-dough for Sunday
mass? Squirting pink icing on pro-life cupcakes? Oh, your
silent choreography, through Chinese pinwheels and
Roman candles. Does our father, the cathedral sacristan,
come in to stare at the two of you with his mouth open
like a dead man? Is Plastic Mary watching the tv that mom
left on with the sound off? Things are bad without you. I'm
reporting to you from the cathedral, where I have been left
with votive candles. The altar looks like a birthday cake
for a corpse. I cannot write you here. You distract me with
Nothing. I will mistake you for small animals furtive in the
undergrowth. I will call out your name while fucking other
bodies, sister, and I will not apologize to them. The tenderness I show them will be yours. I will look over the
white shoulder of a lover who's working hard for my smile
and see you standing calmly at the window. I will bring
thorns home to the one I marry and drop a single rose into
the furnace in silent dedication to you. I cannot betray
you. What do your prayers sound like now? Are they mum-
bled in fatigue by a choir of heavenly boredom? Does an
angel with golden talons and the penis of a dolphin kiss
your wrist which you offer forlornly like an unransomed
princess? Are you dead or am I dreaming your sleep? Blue,
blue skin. Vermiculation is quite an ordinary process.
History? What history? I'm pleading with the present,
here, on my knees in front of the holy present, stroking its
throbbing future like Rick Savage in his fluorescent dressing room. I'm begging to be vulgarized. (The present is
paying to be with me. I'd better show it a good time.) I ask
your permission now, I ask your hope and charity, I ask

your name to unveil me, my mouth parched and bloody with the eating of hourglasses.

Everything has died very nicely in the cathedral court-yard. A car radio plays a Carpenters' tune in the parking lot.

Where are you? Are you between my eye and my throat, deciding whether you will become a tear or a sob? Are you easing some new icon deeper and sweeter up into your pink-white post-shame ache? My room culls light, arranges shadowy bouquets on the wall like those left by an escaping rapist. And you — where do you sleep? Do you rise from your pallet and run a hand through your tangled hair? Do your fingers snag at the base of your neck like the fingers of a braille-reader stopping over a word she doesn't recognize?

I remember you following me into the toilet in the parish hall to watch me pee one spring day. You became captivated by mould on an outtake pipe. You squatted before it for an hour saying *look at the perfection of this,* your voice tuned to the rushing water, the font.

5,

is the number of the Extra Evangelist, you know, the unpublished one.

My five heroes in grade five were John Howard Griffin, Thomas Merton, Beniamino Gigli, Satchel Paige, Josh Gibson. (These last two were the pitcher/catcher nucleus of the Homestead Grays in the 30s. Coal-black, red-eyed — they couldn't read...they didn't know their ages. They played the first night games... setting up magnesium light standards in Texas heat-rash afternoons... tossing and chattering their mockery of Depression-panic with that quiet slave-laughter... striking out those Iowa honkies one by one while the lightning bugs skittered over the corn. Satch used to say I gots three pitches — fast, faster, an fasteress. Josh never said anything.) I warn You, I am beginning to Remember Things. You used to call me names. Once you stuck a safety-pin in my dickhole.

Papers blow across my floor like receipts for embalming.

One summer night Ronnie and I fell asleep in the choir loft. In the morning we woke to cooing from behind the frescoes. We left like vigil-incense through a window, jazzing down Church Street, la dee da, the churches punctuated by beer hall commas, pawn shop colons and clothing exchange equals-signs, the jail and the rooming houses. Past dollar stores crammed with all the Chinese-made toy guns you'd ever need to invade the Tibet pavilion at Disneyworld. The lake bulged like a silicon implant at the south ends of the avenues. We reached the docks and vaulted the fence to board the Toronto Island ferry without paying. The air was hot and we stood palm to palm in empty-bellied defiance of lakewind. The gulls fought over turds bobbing merrily in the harbour.

Back in the cathedral, our sacristan father performed his lonely errands. He topped up the lavabos. He decanted wholesale corn oil from Kansas into little blue bottles the bishop would wave his hand over to authenticate as Holy Land imports so then the blue hairs could sell them after mass like cosmeticians. ("This one, dear, it's just out of this world for bunions..." — "Oh, good gracious, that'll help... now, how about my shingles?")* Yes, Daddy vacuumed the altar, sucking up eucharistic crumbs along with cigarette ash, peeled wax, wick ends, streetmud, encrusted semen∞ from the confessionals, human hair of all colour and thickness, the hoovering muezzin of waste. I imagine that even your hair wound up in his dustbag, Veronica, your raven hair, unworldly suspension above me, always.

---

* Such metaphysical fraud, it seems, may be the most efficient strategy we have against the fraud of reality.

∞ "...As it is strictly forbidden to relieve oneself anywhere save in the chapel, which has been outfitted and intended for this purpose..." — Marquis de Sade, *The 120 Days of Sodom*.

The ferry operators cat-called you from the docks. You frenched me and flipped them the bird over my shoulder.

We disembarked and walked hand in hand. The trees and hedges were varnished in Truth. We looked up. A school of swallows turned in the air to avoid some unseen predator. They moved like the fingerprint of a melting and recomposing man. We came to a maze of hedges erected as a war memorial. The nests of the swallows were there. You said *let's play adam and eve*, and ran ahead of me into the white blossoms. (God knows why we played scriptural games when the rest of our generation was watching tv. It betrays a particular referential desperation. Ya gotta be desperate to play bible games.) I came after you, humouring your inevitable game, plunging into the walls of hidden birds shrieking their congress. You ran like a huntress, or a refugee. Did you know that I just wanted you to stand still so I could stand still and the world could oblige our stillness with a single minute of unchanging light, our bodies an allowance offered to the swallows to sing our peace? Did you know that when I found you in the bush, your white panties with their oval auburn stain hanging from a branch like the skin of a collapsed fruit, I just wanted to watch you touch yourself? Good God, what a sight. You stood balanced as a heron against the cedar brush, your left foot rising to your right knee and tucked upwards to point at your gently behaired centre. Your head thrown up over your shoulder and motionless as though you were observing a star that would disappear before you could turn your body but instead the star held there like an arrowshaft quivering between dark ribs. — You were like a daguerreotype stuck by its corner in a blown-out windowpane in Warsaw, breathing the May breeze, and if I just refocus my eyes for depth I can see the almond blossoms on the rim of that bomb crater. — The weight of your infinite patience against the air. We could still be there if we could master our lives by the magic of stopped breath and conjure the rest of time away. Do you remember a swallow nestling in your palm and your fingers closing around it like a tulip reverse-blossoming and the bird moved not in the cup of your hand while I reached for my tiny cock? Did you know that when I came on the beaten grass that a milky drop fell on your white toe?

Afterwards, we played a dedication game. You led me out of the hedge maze with a swallow feather in your hand and you said

i dedicate this feather to your ears.
I dedicate this stone to your toes.
i dedicate this grassblade to your breath.
I dedicate this grassblade to the strand of hair over your eyes.
i dedicate this grassblade to the bone of your hip.
I dedicate this grassblade to your heel.
i dedicate this grassblade to how your toes spread against the earth.
(pause pause pause) Veronica, I can't think of anything.
c'mon, it's easy. just open your mouth.
I dedicate this grassblade to the innermost whorl of your fingertip, the one they will know you by at the scene of your innocent crime. Ha!
good boy. now, i dedicate this grassblade to the pores in your eyelid through which the photons jostle and make you see blood.
Awright, enough with the grassblades I said.
no. you said, *don't you understand? we are given infinite grassblades to test our languages of gratitude. you're alive, idiot child, you're not allowed to be bored.* [V assumes Jean Harlow pose: hand on hip, furrowed brows...] *boredom is worse than shuishide, kid.*

Then we spent all our money riding the mechanical swans round and around the artificial pond.

6.

All I want is your happiness. Your letter said that you were happy. I imagine you smiling, drifting anonymously through the convent halls like a song on a ghost's Walkman. You wrote about miracles overheard in foreign languages. Olive oil soap. Linen. Your letter sounded like milk. You wrote of angels. *the angels are taking care of me.* They would. The world around you, Veronica, has always been tuned to you: a mongoloid choir behind your rhinestoned platform, the seminarians getting down in their flared epistemologies, thick-veined erections pulsing under the votive bank strobes. The nuns rattle reliquary maracas. The cardinals wear Carmen Miranda hats and twiddle mandolins. You were always able, dear sister, to create everything around you, to make everything into everything else. I think it is raining in Jerusalem.

We played at calvary in the darkened cathedral. You waited for me under station number six, "𝔙𝔢𝔯𝔬𝔫𝔦𝔠𝔞 𝔴𝔦𝔭𝔢𝔰 𝔱𝔥𝔢 𝔣𝔞𝔠𝔢 𝔬𝔣 𝔍𝔢𝔰𝔲𝔰." You were holding a dishcloth outstretched in your small hands. I stumbled to your feet under a hypothetical cross of emotional splinters and theatrical glue. You put the cloth to my face and drew it away. You feigned amazement at my pretended image left there. We froze.* I was uncomfortable in the role of

---

* There is a direct correlation between such frozen tableaux of memory and the growing suspicion that we are shadows locked into eroding histories. It's almost as if we leave facades of our bodies behind in strong memories, rendering current existences thinner and thinner. I am reminded of the colour plates used to assemble colour prints. Let us say my Image can be divided into many such plates. If a memory is strong enough, one of those plates is peeled away from the Image to support the structural weight of that memory, in much the same way that an architect, for example, who is commissioned to add an addition to an old building may have to use materials meant for the new building (upon which there is a fixed spending limit) to bolster the old, the integrity of which he has violated by his very presence. The emotional expenditures of memory, therefore, steal colour away from the present, in order to reveal the truth of the Black beneath what we know as Now.

Christ, as most romantics secretly are.

The moon shone through the clerestory like a blindfolded choirboy singing a painfully high note while a deacon sucks him off.

I associate you with birds, sister. Mainly from this one scene. It happened after I had started playing the pipe organ and you were fucking every boy in the parish. You came with me one day to watch me practice. You asked me to show you the pipes. We climbed ladders and opened small doors. (Such human activities.) You shed your winter clothes. Your immaculate flesh craned in the pipelined vault. Your coat your dress your tights your bra your panties hanging each from the mouth of a pipe like laundry in an ossuary. Your nipples as cold and hard as the glassbead stamen heads spattering the rose window. You said *leave me here, go around to the console and play, and i will fly to keep myself warm.*

I believe I played a Bach fugue. *Fugue* means escape. A highly repetitive, self-imitative form, so precise in formalistic convention that it can be easily improvised.

7.

Confession is an old pattern for me. It seems to be necessary politics amidst crumbling things.

8.

What follows is the first of many brief **m e t a f i c — t i o n a l   p a r a b l e s**, most of which are positioned after some personal commentary such as is found in #7. Notice how the following shift to the **t h i r d   p e r s o n v o i c e** gives a new **o u t e r   a u t h o r i t y** to the reflection. I tell parables, sister, in the hope of teaching myself about myself by pretending I am **o u t s i d e** of myself. Someday I will actually **b e l i e v e** that there is a

distance between **naming** myself as "**I**", and as "**h e**", and that distance is the **m e a s u r e** of the **Truth** I long for like a respectable businessman longs to be lashed by the **penis-whips** of his dominatrix **whore**. Unfortunately, both "he" and "I" will be dead then, long since sucked into the **Truth-Vacuum** between them.

Once upon a time there was a boy who went to confession to hear himself recount the events of his life. The priest was unnecessary, for the boy acknowledged absence as his true confessor. In the blue glow of Absence, self-Surveillance was his Sacrament.

He kept himself company with the recital of his memories. Every confession was like a walk in low tide where certain shells begged to be grasped and placed to the ear or blown through like a conch that called the world out of slime in a mythology that remained "primitive" because it reminded certain bankers and their fat wives that they were made of shit. Eventually, this contemplation of shells would tire him. He would finish confessing, and then assign himself the arbitrary penance of continuing with his life. He would step out from behind the curtain. The tide came in with the folds returning. The ungathered shells washed away. He would have to travel to find them. Or someone else would gather them and confess a beautiful genesis through muck and pearl, saying *this is where I came from*, and, by saying this, would create truth. Shells and events belong to no one.

(The world forces human voices to confess its sins for it. Humans die because this discipline consumes their flesh. Soon there is no one left to confess for the world and the world falls mute like a severed windpipe exhaling onto the stone floor of temple ruins.)

The boy confessed to step out of his life like a tear. He wrote his name in many places. Everything had a surface and the surfaces begged to be touched. He mimed many bodies in gestures towards the future, leaving his own body in prayerful pastcoming stasis. Many bodies turned away from him to gaze downwards. One by one, his organs were transplanted in Catholic hospitals during bouts of hypochondria. The nursing nuns paid little attention to blood types and infections. He sewed many costumes of scars to hide his scars, which would be traced by strange tongues when strangers licked him. He waded through the stories he had spilled. They evaporated as if from the petri dishes of failed fertilization experiments. They rained on him again, now mingled with salt. He lived the same moment. Over and over he lived. Wind passed through. The sky lactated just enough to engage his sucking reflex, and then no more. He ran his tongue over horizon. He swallowed to destroy detail. History was digested. Wood burned in its crosses. Absence was his perfect returning. The side of his body facing the shadows opened. He turned twelve. (His sister was somewhat older, and knew his confessions before he spoke them.)

9.

O Veronica will lay down beside me and I will make my confession to her. My confession will not say *I am a confession*. My confession will not say *I*. Nor will it be a monologue. Nor will it carry the romance of originality. Nor will it be any more interesting than soil. Nor will it be applauded by a surrogate of **God's infinite audience**. Nor will it be **conditional**. Nor will it be concerned with **context**. Nor will it fill a requirement of lovers unmet by touching. Absence will recreate the body out of everything the body lacked. The Perfect Litany of History will be sung by a ghostly choir and recorded on wax cylinders improvised from Easter candles. There will be no possessions. So possessed, Veronica will lay down beside me. There will be no **s h a d o w t h e a t r e** of touching. She will listen to me. And her listening will be my disappearance. And my disappearance will believe its **w o r d s .** And these are the **w o r d s** it will say: _____, _____-_____, and _____.

Once we stole two old chalices from the sacristy. We drilled holes in the cups. We tied string between them and this was our weird tin-can telephone. We could whisper to each other from great distances. You standing in grotto to the Virgin, and me in the confessional as always.

It worked fine when you were around, Veronica. But now the chalices are good for nothing. They won't even hold wine anymore. I haven't checked to see if they will hold blood. — Who the hell would want these? the pawnbroker said. I looked over his shoulder and saw the shelf stacked with Charlie's Angels lunchboxes, selling for fifty bucks apiece.

10.

Pare the wick on this Nicaraguan-sweatshop made Eternalux™ candle guaranteed for 300 hours of no-drip meditative burning. On one side a picture of St. Anthony* holding a lamb in crook of his arm, other hand grasping staff wedged into cleft rock from which pastel water flows. On the other side within scarlet regal frame is printed

Prayer to St. Anthony
to be say many time for all good things:

O Saint Anthony, who by you passion and bloody
showed the Faces of the Christ to many poors peoples
please help me in the despairs and fix my black heart
in your talkings to the God.
O Saint Anthony let me remember how holy you look
as the shepherd of all sinners here in the teary vale.
I ask especially that you help me with
(name your desirings)
and keep praying to for me to see the God.

and as I light this candle on the eleventh day of my captivity, let me remember the desirings that my sister Veronica listed. She wrote on a yellow pad

---

*When the tomb of St. Anthony was opened in 1263 in the presence of St. Bonaventure, it was seen that his body had decomposed. His tongue, however, was intact. The tongue is still kept in a reliquary in the treasury of the basilica of Sant' Antonio in Padua. Make of this what you will. I imagine the good monks feeding it Tic Tacs donated by pilgrims with vinyl sunhats. I imagine crazy old widows in black trying to french it through the glass. I imagine when the church bells toll over the ruins it wriggles and curls and flicks itself limpidly around the vowels of old prayers.

desirings for the st. anthony candleflame:

- to meet mother teresa and tell her what it feels like to have your earlobe sucked by a boy whose name you don't care to know

- to learn to smoke cigarettes with my vagina and contract my womb to puff the smoke at the cameraman and cloud his porno eye

- to be prettier

- if not prettier, then to be a boy

- to be a boy with a constantly erect cock

- to seduce a jesuit who is trying to absolve me

- to seduce a benedictine nun who is fitting me for a habit

- to have a metal breastplate like joan of arc with deadly tit-cones

- to become a famous painter of icons and illuminator of scripture who eats cadmium and goes mad with great uproar in a european scriptorium

- to learn how to love perfectly

She ripped the page from the pad and tore it to shreds. We went back to writing our Lenten reflections for Fr. Oldgrave's class. Outside, the March snow clung to the mud like the pellets of styrofoam that padded our Atari console in its shiny cardboard box.

11.

Veronica your genius held a knife at my white throat and said sing.

We slipped from our rooms together on Easter Monday and rooted through the trash for the sucked bones of the turkey mom bought for a penny a pound by lining up out-

side Ed Mirvish's garish funhouse store at four in the
morning on April 14, feast of St. John Chrysostom. Mom
stood under chaser lights looping imported plastic shoes,
polyester blankets made in Armenian sweatshops, cosmetic
for faces and kitchen floors lined up like shooting gallery
prizes behind streaked glass. She stood shivering in her
frumpy grey skirt, stamping her feet in brown vinyl flats.
— She never knew how to dress... I fantasize that she was
pretty once: Dad groping a perky breast in 1958 through
her lemon Betty Grable strapless swimsuit on a daytrip to
Hanlan's Point, Mom getting all mortified and blushing
like a peach under her orange-ribboned straw hat, Dad
shrugging and flopping over to stretch out on the sand and
watch B-52s fly cold war manoeuvres over Lake Ontario,
while Mom checks her Woolworth's lipstick in her compact... it all makes me so sad. — On Easter night,
Veronica slipped into my bed and held me close. She said
you know what we should do?
What?
we should ressurect the butterball
We scrounged in trash, up to our elbows. The April
night wore its late frost like a Victorian housewife feigning
consumption... in the early moon all the homeless had
fallen thawed onto the pavement from where they'd been
frozen upside down into the trunks of splitting trees. We
wrapped the bones in newspaper. We did this for a week
until the leftovers were gone. We fought off starving rac-
coons with hockey sticks.

Mother saved the wishbone, leaving it to dry over the
sink. She insisted that we break it between ourselves. We
did. You won. Mom applauded and rationed out Smarties
in pathetic congratulations. She said *what did you wish for,
darling?* and you replied with a sweet smile *happiness in
our catholic home.* Later I asked What did you really
wish for, Ronnie? and you said *shhh*

We cut school and stole money from the cathedral poor
box and boarded a northbound bus with drunken lumber-

jacks and scarfaced Mohawks and rejects from the Marlies headbanging to Judas Priest and AC/DC. The bag of turkey bones under the seat. Up through rows of prefab bungalows and trailer homes plunked in the swamps like car-shaped candles on nursing home birthday cakes... industrial encampments sinking into the marshy earth... a universe of abandoned farmhouses and barns slumped like autopsy snapshots thrown from the window of a Studebaker hearse.... How silent you were in the aisle seat until your arm raised across my eyes to point at the window and you said *this vignette is brought to you by heritage canada.* The streaks of dried rain on the glass made the world look like a handheld video shot by tourists to a half-reality. We got off at Marylake, where the Augustinians live with their cows and hymnbooks. You told me that in times of war monasteries have been the perennial choice of fugitives and terrorists for cover. *likewise, we need refuge for our poor bird here* you said, lifting up the plastic Toys R Us bag, which was beginning to stink.

(Veronica, where are you? Have you wiped your menstruation with leaves and left them in piles for the rats to lick as you walk away slowly, pleased by the logic of things?)

We wrapped the bones in the fishnet stocking you found in a Parkdale alleyway one Sunday morning while the whores slept in the tenements above like cats in the branches of necropolis oak. We stepped off the shoulder and into the brush.

Birds called out, wanting to be noticed by you, to fit into the vista of your plan. A single chestnut fell from a tree with a tiny thud. The reeds barred our eyes from the twentieth century. We waded through the marsh and passed a tool shed in a vine-sheathed clearing. Beside it, a heap of compost iced with guano buzzed with greenbacked flies. You gave me the bones to hold and rolled up your sleeves and sank your hands into the base of the mound, augering a niche for our package. You stuffed it in and sealed it up. The larvae wriggled on your forearms in the dun light. The bells from the monastery rang out like iron trash barges bumping gently in New York Harbour. You washed your arms in a murky stream.

We hopped the next city bus. I slept with my head in your lap. You bent over me... maybe my eyelid fluttered... your flesh, a nipple touching my cheek... your sweater... a dream of rubber tires... acrylic can pass for angora... now there is light... the bones on the compost-lobe... my attention... the retrieval... that peace before consummation...

12.

There are twelve Fruits of the Spirit. There are twelve gates and foundation stones in the Holy City. Each gate is named for a fruit. Each fruit is named for its seed. Each seed is named for its dream. I have no idea if this is true. I am making things up because I am convinced that everything should be significant. There were twelve words in my last confession: "I committed incest with my sister because I thought she was God."

13.

Veronica we walked to the Parkdale dump to do what you called **r e s e a r c h**. We saw a cat give birth in the shell of an old **t e l e v i s i o n**. Half of its litter was **s t i l l b o r n**. You said *look – a tabernacle.*

14.

LADIES AND GENTLEMEN, WE WILL NOW ATTEND TO CREATION. EXHAUSTED STEWARDS,

WATCH THE CORMORANTS FLY LOW, THEIR
WINGS HEAVY WITH OIL. BE NOURISHED BY THE
NATURAL ICONS OF THE WORLD. HONEY AND
LOCUSTS FOR EVERYONE. REMEMBER BLUE
AFTERNOONS OF RAIN IN DISTANT CHILD-
HOODS, KNEELING ON A RAG RUG ON THE BACK
PORCH, WATCHING THE VERTICAL LITURGY,
PLUMB LINE OF SACRIFICE, THE WATER IN THE
MESH SCREEN BELLING THOUSANDS OF LENSES
MINISCULE AND TEMPORARY, THROUGH WHICH
THE GARDEN SWELLS IN HOLOGRAM BEFORE
YOU. THE RAIN KISSES YOUR FOREHEAD WITH
AUTISTIC GRACE. MARK THE SLOW WEEPING OF
VEGETATION INTO ITS OWN CORE. THE ROOT-
BOUND CRUST IS A CROSS SECTION OF FLESH
TRANSVERSED BY THREE DIMENSIONAL CALLIG-
RAPHY. KNOW THAT THIS MEMORIAL PHAN-
TASM EXISTS ONLY TO PROVIDE A WHOLLY
IMPERFECT MEANS FOR THE WORLD TO TALK
ABOUT ITSELF RINGING LONELY. KNOW THAT
THERE IS ORDER HERE, OBSCURED ONLY BY
YOUR EFFORT TO UNVEIL IT. KUANOS. BLACK
GLASS. YOUR SEEKING MIND PART OF THE HOR-
RIFIC MYSTERY, YOUR THINKING LIKE A SPREAD-
ING STAIN. THE WORLD IS A MACHINE USED TO
RECORD YOUR RESPONSE TO ITSELF. JESUS
CHRIST IS LOOKING AT YOUR BRAIN WITH
TONGUE DEPRESSORS. EVERYTHING IN THE
IMAGE OF A HUMAN, TOUCHING ITSELF.
OBSERVE THE SEPULCHRE OF ROCK, ITS CRYS-
TALLIZED ORGANS. OBSERVE YOUR HAND, ITS
WEALTH OF MINERALS PARALLELED ONLY BY
ITS NATURAL LACK OF INTEREST IN ECONOMY.
LEAVE THE HIGHWAY AND MAKE LOVE TO A
LAVA FLOW WITH THE GRACE OF YOUR TWIST-
ING METAL. YOU HAVE NOWHERE ELSE TO GO,
WHY PRETEND YOU DO. WRITE A POEM ABOUT

TORNADOES. RESEARCH THE SUBLIME. WHEN YOU HAVE FINISHED, BEGIN AGAIN, READING ALL THE BOOKS BACKWARDS. REMEMBER THE WORDS OF THE APOSTLE CONCERNING THE GROANING OF A WORLD IN DELIVERANCE. PRE-PARE FOR POST-PARTUM DEPRESSION, PLACEN-TAL SCHIST. MAKE A DESK OF CEDARWOOD, PUT IT ON THE PORCH OF A THATCHED HUT IN THE FOREST, FALL ASLEEP THERE EVERY DAY AT THREE O'CLOCK. DREAM OF DIVINE CIRCULA-TION. THERE ARE NO NEWSPAPERS IN HEAVEN. SEE A FAWN URINATE ON A DRIFT OF ROTTING LEAVES. WONDER AT THE TECHNOLOGIES OF FLIGHT. WIPE LANOLIN FROM YOUR BROW. MOURNING IN THIS VALLEY: AUDITORIUM. ORGAN MUSIC. THAT WHICH GIVES HOPE WHERE DEATH IS GREEDY WITH THE LAN-GUAGE. ORGANIC THEATRE, THE TRAGEDY OF APRIL RIVULETS ON THE MOUNTAINSIDE, WHERE THE RAM LOSES FOOTING AND THEIR WORM ENTERS THE THIGHS OF HEROES. EXHAUSTED STEWARDS ALL, YOU HAVE BEEN RUNNING AFTER SOMETHING AS STILL AS THE FIVE FACES OF NOVEMBER. HERE ARE SOME STICKS FOR YOUR ALTAR. WIPE UP THE BLOOD WHEN YOU ARE FINISHED OR THE WOLVES WILL KNOW TO COME FOR YOUR CHILDREN.

15.

Veronica, you were twelve years old and knew far more than liver-spotted priests who waste over the onionskin midrashim of their own solipsism, who fall asleep scrub-bing god's dentures with the bristly pubes of self-righteous virginity.

Once you counted the grains of sand that represented three minutes. Do you remember wrapping the egg timer in newspaper and breaking it softly in your hands like the neck of a hummingbird? Do you remember counting the grains, picking each one up out of its bed of newsprint with mom's eyebrow tweezers? Do you remember showing me how some grains rested in the loops of World News Digest letters that closed on themselves like windowframes: A, D, g, O, P, Q, R? You counted all day. It took thirteen hours to examine the silicate machinery of three minutes. You said there were seven thousand six hundred and eighty-nine grains of white sand in three minutes. You continued your calculations on the margins of newsprint, beside ads for stripjoints and sofas. You wrote

3 minutes = 7689 grains of sand
times 20 for an hour = 153780
times 24 for a day = 3690720
times 365 for a year = 1347112800
times 75 for a life = 101033460000 = the number of grains on an average beach, assuming regular tides and no extraneous human development such as oil well excavation or the building of shipping docks, also assuming no human disasters such as shipwrecks or abandoned driftnets, all in all taking into account only natural nonhuman things : sandpipers, burrowing clams, gulls, etc.

Then you said something that I can't quite remember about dolphins washing up upon the beaches of our time. You said they die of cancer because they love to nuzzle up against the warm metal of ejected rocket boosters. This gives them tumours in their brains like diamonds.

16.

This is turning into your Gospel, Veronica. Let it open like the Gospel of Thomas, like this: These are the secret sayings of Jesus Christ spoken in solitude and recorded by His brother…

St. Elizabeth of Hungary dies in 1231. At her wake, an hysteric peasant broke through the brown line of Dominican bouncers and rushed the corpse. It was all laid out in state with garlands of bougainvillea and sachets of lavender in her armpits. The guy bit off her cold blue nipples and fled the cathedral with them crumbling in his mouth. Shortly thereafter, he was struck down by the pox. Elizabeth, however, bled from her breasts forever. His bites had proven her incorruptible.

17.

hey lemur evil ambergris thelor deswith I was sure that by the time I was eight I had prayed as many rosary beads as would replace the volume of my body. I imagined unhooking the little metal chains to let the beads flow into my shell. *eeble essay dart thong wee mammon.* I grew in size and weight because I enlarged my body to hold more prayer, making additions with twigs, plastic packaging, dust, broken ceramics, the ooze from a punctured Stretch Armstrong. *bleedes theft route of die room creases.*

Nouns were severed body parts repairing their wounds through verbs. Each cell was a bead and my blood was a loop of words tied together. The loop tightened when I prayed the words faster. *soul amaris, motheat of god prefer us innards.* When it didn't make sense for my blood to remain in drops, my blood and the words ran themselves together in phrases bridged by *and.* Now, when it doesn't make sense for my body to remain in flesh, it dissolves along the faultlines of devotion, bridged by nothing, for I am gone. *no wand acme whore of whore death**

Veronica taught me how to pray by pushing me through her magical verbal sieves. *distrust victorian rhetoric! you yelled unbury the rose of devotion from the shitpile of ecclesial pedants!* She pushed me from the precipice of Catholic Style. I slipped like a stillbirth plunging from snowdrift to snowdrift on a ridged mountain. I prayed:

hail mary full of grace the lord is with thee blessed art thou among women and blessed is the fruit of thy womb jesus holy mary mother of god pray for us sinners now and at the hour of our death

When I hit the first drift the crystals of ice formed a tessellated fishnet that snagged the nouns and names from my prayer, catching them like bricks stolen from pillaged ruins. These were the heaviest words, and without them I should have fallen less quickly — my body, however, like any dead weight, gained speed. She told me to say the prayer again:

hail full of the is with blessed art among and blessed is the of thy holy of pray for now and at the of our

I plunged through the second drift, a gold-digger's pan, its holes small enough to catch the modifiers of my prayer, which had been attached to the nouns like robotic hands holding paintbrushes on an assembly line of forgeries. She told me to say the prayer again:

---

*"The syncope signifies both a temporary interruption of a body's consciousness, the suppression of a letter or syllable within a word, and the liaison of the last note of a measure of music with the first note of the next measure to make them appear to be one single note." — Louis Marin — *Le récit est un piège*, Paris: Minuit, 1978.

hail of the is with art and is the of of pray for and at the of

The third drift was a flour sieve plucking out the definite articles which had been forced to point at the nouns they were enslaved by, in order to falsely root the names in the bread oven of time and space. She told me to say the prayer again:

hail of is with art and is of of pray for and at of

The fourth drift was a linen funeral sheet. Its tightly knit fabric squeezed the curd of connectives away from my language, the of's and and's and for's and at's that pretend to hold meaning together. She told me to say the prayer again:

hail is art is pray

The final drift was a sheet of fine parchment. I thought my body would tear it. But I had dissolved, and my particles slipped through the weave of grain and pulp. This last layer removed the final stain of my prayer, which was no longer mine. It turned the exclamatory of address into pigment, and absorbed it as ink into its pores. After I passed through it, this sheet became a one-word missive, an exuberant "Hail" addressed to no one and unsigned, therefore written by everyone, to be sent to everyone. She told me to say the prayer again:

is art is pray

The prayer had become perfect through her teaching. All that remained were the verbs, which meant that it could recite itself. I had no strength to repeat it. I had retained just enough consciousness to think about when and where I would hit bottom. Then I realized that bottom was a noun, and I had lost my ability to say or understand nouns many levels ago, before I knew you fully, Veronica, when I saw my body through only the most distorted mirrors of my language.

It was my first lesson in editing.

18.

Which way do I face to prostrate myself towards Jerusalem? Do I turn towards the Good Shepherd Refuge? Community Outreach Detox Drop-In? The bombed abortion clinic on Harbord Street? Rue Ste-Catherine in Montreal? Towards Glace Bay? St. John's? Gander? Greenland? Red lights in Amsterdam? A slaughterhouse under an apartment block in Cairo? Do I face Auschwitz? Where is my Mecca? Is it your turkey skeleton, Veronica, varnished and primed for museum flight? (So many unfinished stories...) Is it the hull of the old family station wagon, rusting to oblivion in a Riverdale junkyard? Can we ever again trust the compass in the plastic womb of the dashboard Mary? Why are all the mapmakers munching Cheese Doodles as they sit palely in front of underground computer screens looking at the world through secret communion with whizzing satellites? Is this what honourable exploration has become? Is this the noble adventure? Where is de Chardin with his haloed pith helmet? Where is the inviolated tabernacle? Where is the rat-free library? Where is the chapel that is not attached to a gift shop?

Where is that picture of you, Veronica, standing under the cherry blossoms?

Veronica, I have decided this. We grew up like pavement weeds feeding in the cathedral downspout. You taught me heliotropic contortionism. We had a mother and father but we were parented by a sucking historical Absence. They were supernumeraries in your fabulous medieval film. Mother stoked the scullery fire. Father wheeled the dead-cart. Let me narrate his absence in particular, for in this deep night I am plagued not only by the flower of your mouth but by his scapular of blackened tongues.

Our father was the sacristan of Saint Michael's Cathedral. Important job. Keys to the tabernacle and the Bishop's Caddie when it needed to be parked or waxed. Much head nodding and demure shuffling. The Cathedral is the seat of the Toronto Archdiocese. Blessed by Bishop Michael Power in 1883. An ambrotype hangs in the vestibule: Power is standing in a crowd of craggy, tubercular Irish holding pickaxes, he's blessing the cornerstone with a little silver wand. A detonating box sits in the foreground like a mushroom. Thirty-two workers were killed in its construction; no union to care for their widows or bastards. The Cathedral is a Keeper of a True Cross Relic which looks like two toothpicks from Sammy Woo Chinese Restaurant on Dundas. Boasts a baptismal registry of 94 leatherbound volumes. It is located on the corner of Shuter and Bond. Surrounded by Metropolitan United Church, St. James Anglican Cathedral, Ryerson Polytechnical Institute, Legion Hall 778, Moss Park Armoury, Le Strip Burlesque, the Zanzibar, Victory Rooming House, Adelaide Street Detox Centre, and Covenant House Shelter. Past patron of Saint Michael's Hospital, where in 1946, Mrs. Eva McIsaac, a part Huron housewife from Uptergrove between Lakes Simcoe and Couchiching was examined continually for two weeks by Protestant doctors who assured the international press that she was a bona fide stigmatist who bled every Friday between 6 and 9 in the evening. One block east of Massey

Hall, venue of many famous artists and speakers:
Beniamino Gigli, the Lourdes children, Glenn Gould,
Caruso, Andreas Segovia, Emma Goldman, Edward
MacMillan, Sarah Vaughan, Thelonius Monk with
Charlie Mingus, Aretha Franklin, Betty Friedan, and
Gordon Lightfoot. Two blocks west lies the stupendous
Eaton Centre, a necker-cube kaleidoscope of shopping
bliss completed in 1976, in which one shop sells souvenir
plastic repros of most of the aforementioned buildings to
vacationing industrialists from Georgia who all say 'Well,
I'll be durned. This city is so damned clean!' but get
annoyed when blacks show up in the crosshairs of their
camcorders. The Cathedral was presided over during our
childhood by Cardinal Gerald Emmett Carter who had
trouble elevating the communion host because of paralysis
in his left side. I think he was a nice guy, I can't remember. Saint Michael's Cathedral is now the seat of
Archbishop Aloysius Ambrozic, who's absolutely con-
vinced that every queer and feminist in this town is working for the KGB or Satan.

Our Father worked at this church seven days a week, had
lunch at Raffle's Burgers on Thursdays and drank pitchers
of Molson Ex at the Imperial Public Library Tavern,
watching the Leafs through the thin years. He had the
records of Sam Cooke and Nina Simone and Nat King
Cole. We were given free room and subsidized board and
use of a 1970 lime-green Dodge Dart with black vinyl inte-
rior and an honorarium of about four grand a year, all in
all totalling an annual Cathedral tax-break of about
$5,872. We were a Share Life/St. Vincent de Paul family.

It was Our Father's custom to steal unconsecrated wine.
— There he is, swigging away by the baptismal font, tottering under the moonlight like a trained seal. — There
he is, passed out on his knees in the last pew.— Staggering
through the stations of the cross, his bottle hipslung, regarding the molded plaster calvary with the nostalgia of a
Prisoner allowed to tour the Jail built for Him alone.

Encircling the nave, his eyesight winewashed and bloody, stopping by a bank of votive candles at a side altar. Veronica, do you remember how we once played at guessing the name of the corpse for whom each particular flame danced? I chose saints' names. You chose the names of the strippers you'd seen on the Brass Rail marquee.

Dad moves away. He drinks. He stops for a moment to cry rosé. He draws back a curtain and kneels in a confessional. He is silent. After a while, he backs out of the stall and enters the priestly side and sits on the pillowed chair and imagines listening to the sins of strangers. Both stalls look the same, with velvet rims. He belches. He is silent. I could write "Again, he is silent", Veronica, but what two silences are the same? How can I ever again assume monotony, I who learned from you to regard the epiphanies latent in boredom? Our father is leaving the stall, bottle in hand. He weaves a fretless loomwork. He farts. The altar now... he genuflects out of habit... no taking chances under the Gaze... fear and silence masking a burning heart. See how he mounts the sanctuary steps, runs a hand along the marble altartop to coerce a suspicion of warmth from the relic he believes to be buried within it. Cathedral of St. Michael the Archangel Whose Altar Contains a True Relic in the Form of a Bone from the Wing of Our Great Patron. You told me this was bullshit, Veronica, you told me to distrust any reliance on the impossible. But then you said *all the same, don't think it's not holy, little one, don't think that because the fucking bones of an angel wing aren't lodged in this upscale butchery block that all this is a fraud. things are made holy by random social contract. our sickly hearts are moved by third rate fireworks. things are made holy by the accumulated superstition of the illiterate. this is good. worship this relic, little one. commend yourself to the beliefs of the stupid. if you suspect it to be a chicken bone then worship it care about the* bone and then don't care about the bone and then care about the bone again. the angel's in your head. close your eyes and study him be a disciple to his foreign glory. our father believed the relic. he was a believer in bigger lies than our own.

He moves from the altar and stands under the sanctuary lamp like a blind man in a baroque frieze, half-hidden by the dress-folds of a Titian Salome. See how he kneels on the double kneeler like a bridegroom unsurprised at being jilted because he always knew the nice young girl would fall for the yuppie with hidden deSadean impulses in the end. See how he looks through the tabernacled light for any sign of your white dress, Ronnie.

His unknown visions fail as the morning approaches, bell-ringing time. He limps to the door of the choir loft with skeleton keys rattling at his belt and he climbs the spiral staircase to emerge like an apparition under the rose window which is gaining a dull lightbound colour like cotton gauze patted to a damp wound. He shoves the sloshing bottle into his belt and swings up onto the rope ladder tethered to a beam in the belltower. He climbs like an arthritic spider up and through the trapdoor in the roof of the loft. He pulls himself through and squats panting on the highslung boards. He staggers to his feet. He retrieves the bottle and uncorks it and swigs deeply and replaces the cork and rams it home with the heel of his hand. He holds the wine in his mouth and turns to look out of the belltower window. The city lies like a busted tv seen through a junkshop window; its severed cords are sparking as gently as the neurons of the beheaded... tarpaulins propped up on broken hockey sticks in the alleyways like makeshift greenhouses for all things in human ferment... rancid steam rising from the subway vents through the happy mandinkas of punkers seeking warmth... the ponderous circulation of garbage and bread and milk trucks with cab doors opening for thin men to dismount and place ambiguous gifts at the doorsteps of barred shops before climbing back in to the sound of the mischanneled radio to resume the trek through concrete limbs... wanderers by the lake-front who slip tenderly into low-ceilinged diners as though awakened from a decade-long dream and meekly suspicious of the possibility of warmth and food... greasy-jeaned Ojibwa warriors lined up in front of the Sally Ann regarded by elderly women on the way to dawn mass carrying tiny purses rattling with coppers and hairpins and crochet hooks... lone scribes drinking black coffee from paper cups attempting parallel conjurations of a world that seems on occasion to weave like grapevine and carillon wire and thus TRANSCENDS by way of breathless syntax... and remnants of nonhuman orders... those few trees of great age preserved in city parks... horizon whose marring would come undone if the city were to vanish into the lake... He looks down to the digital clock suspended outside the funeral home and awaits his sign. The clock blinks 6:00 into puddles. Alarms sound in hidden rooms, waking those with beds and reasons to rise. Automatic coffee makers turn themselves on in the suburbs while radios receive lists of catastrophes and doorcrashers. Women bend over rigourously in spandex and legwarmers and men light first cigarettes. Refugees cross themselves or prostrate eastwards. Pale night-shift nurses and smeared whores perfumed by unfamiliar yet unsurprising secretion draw back the deadbolts to their shitty apartments and commence the running of baths. — Love is near. — Veronica, Our Father surveys this panorama with an eyeglass made of broken wings. And now the sudden burst of fury, hurling the empty bottle down the carillon shaft where it smashes among the broken and abandoned nests of birds, reaching for the bellrope with hands blueveined and cramped and leaps into space and lashes his meatless thighs around the coil and lets the weight of his body swing the bell above into high clamour against itself, ringing and ringing and ringing like cadmium angelcum to call them to worship, to call us to worship, to call them all to worship, those he loves who are lodged in his mind like bright potsherds recovered from cities now siltpacked, and those he despises who burrow in blind spots like demons he will never name.

19.

Somewhere my sister breathes the sun through a convent window. She pauses and looks up from a prayer book. She wakes up naked in clean linens, and wonders where I am. A single bird sings a tender mercy. It will die. Mercy will die. Singing will die. Singularity will die. Tenderness will be stored for a moment in my heart and then I will die. O God, let the moment of my leaving this room have been planned for a thousand years. Let the smallest movement of my hand in the air fulfill a burnt piece of scripture. Let every wasted spermatozoa in this bedsheet wriggle out a grateful dance of freedom before it dies in the cold. (Let the rapist pause at the rain. Let him pick up earth. Let him pause and wonder at the segmented back. Let him envision a garden. Let him open the door of a birdcage made with chicken bones. Let him help a single mother on the subway with her pram. Let him watch the spring gather smoke. Let me leave him to his own unlikely reparation.) Let the prayer pray me. Let the newspaper lady warm her face in her dirty scarf. Let the traffic stop with the coagulation of oil wells. Let me wake up speaking Hebrew. Let the bellringer balance on the bell trestle before swinging. Let time remind itself of sleeping. Let that dream be erased and the paper folded up. Let the midnight bather mime baptism and be surprised by a warm undertow but unsurprised by the corpse brushing against her thin white arm.

20.

A Self-Mythologizing Fable:

Once the Boy of Probable Beginnings began to touch himself, he understood absence to be his true and perfect lover.

He did not fantasize form but vistas. His desire rose towards horizons and ranges. He could only fulfil himself by contemplating what lay beyond retinal limitation. In his mind he walked through the folds of matter. (Humans are burrowing creatures in sex and their burrowing produces more humans to seek and provide provisional foldings of heart and flesh and mind.) He came over visions of oceans. He came over mountains, shelves of books, leaves, folios, signatures he could burrow himself in, covetous of celestial alphabets.

Sometimes, his body was a prosthetic to a world wanting to love itself. Sometimes, his body was a scar betraying the world's masochistic fetishes.

His self-love kept him primed for his sister, it kept him lean and hungry. He learned his body only to be able to offer it to her.

The first time he died was when he touched his finger to his tongue and his finger was wet with semen. The fluid was living, moving to complete itself against Probable Deaths. He thought of eating himself to feed his absence and animate the dream of Possible Histories now wriggling upon his lips. The taste was somehow familiar. The Boy could either spit or swallow. The room was cold. His mother arranged her hair in the mirror behind his bedroom wall. It began to rain. He swallowed. Destiny tasted like air trapped in the bellows of an abandoned pipe organ.

He slept fitfully that night, as though he were being frigged by a ghost.

He lived to contain. He contained to break. He broke to spill. He spilled to seed. He seeded to die. He died to say

Veronica
towards
you

I
pull
myself
off

this page
this page
this page
this page
this page

amen

,

21.

Veronica, I watched you get fucked outside against the stone wall under the barred window depicting the Presentation in the Temple. I never saw his face and so I remember him as you do because your eyes were closed. Let it suffice to say that he was worshipping. I said nothing because you said nothing. You bent forward, corseted with anima, picking oilpaint weeds from a nineteenth century garden. Your ass was a white seaflower nudged by hormonal undercurrents. (Image from cinema history: Raven-haired Bardot plays St. Bernadette while Orson Welles hangs from theatre cables with Cecil B. DeMille putting out cigars on his ass.) He thrusted behind you and grunted without grace. I saw you begin to shake gently as though you were rooted and water gushed past your tubers underground. You bit your lip. I understand this now as your orgasm, the first I witnessed. You did not call out but arched like a slow acrobat on a trapeze. He cried like a stabbed thing. He withdrew and the condom slid from his purple cock. You remained facing away. Your abdomen contracted as he slapped your ass in goodbye. He wiped the drool from his chin with the back of his hand. He disappeared through the alleyway garbage. You turned to gaze at the sky like Teresa of Avila watching the beginning of a rainfall on a verdant hillside while in the village below gypsy musicians strike up an ancient quadrille. Thank God your imagination healed everything, sister, or was it mine? I stuffed my entire hand down my craw to wrest loud sobs from your beatified audition. You broke your trance, pulled up your tights and followed him out into the city. I approached your dissolving altar. I knelt. I picked up the condom and tilted out the semen. I put it to my face to smell for you. It smelt of latex and that acrid liquor I have come to know. As always, you had disappeared. I would come to expect this, knowing that to approach a crystal makes its prism invisible to the naked begging eye. I dropped the condom into a dumpster which was filled with rotting plaster and wooden moldings carved with cherubs that had surrounded the altar inside. At that time the diocese was renovating the cathedral to prepare for the arrival of the Pope.

22.

Who was that man, Veronica? I asked.
   shhhh you said.

23.

I am 23 years old.

24.

Who was that man, Veronica? I asked.
   shhhh you said, drawing the sound from your thymus out and it flowered around your face like a veil, like all your language flowing from the open end of a catheter tube held like Narcissus' straw in a pool of clear water so everything that hid you appeared as a cloud of blood-flavoured Tang dissipating in a Holiday Inn swimming pool like a rose imagined.

25.

Veronica, I watched you receive an abortion against the stone wall under the barred window depicting the Presentation in the Temple. I never saw his face and so I remember him as you do because your eyes were closed. Let it suffice to say that he was worshipping. I said nothing because you said nothing. You arched backward, corseted with anima, reaching for oilpaint hanging vines in a nineteenth century garden. (Image from cinema history: Diamanda Galas playing Joan of Arc with crotchless armour while Ingrid Bergman struggles in her dressingroom with a leather truss and her lush red mouth sealed with

---

The Abortion! The Abortion! O sweet God The Abortion! Call the theorists! Call the camera crews! Ask serious questions! Gather the insights of the bewildered! Argue the definitions of sentience and personhood with the confidence of Waldorf teachers! The pilgrims rush forward. They cry out. They are rebutted. The pilgrims wave their petitions in Sunday Offering envelopes. The pilgrims call for sacrifice and statistics. Visualize blood! Type O negative! Type: "O -"! Look at the trash can and count the little skulls! The doctors shake their starched heads. A tear falls from the eye of menstruant nurse. The protesters salute before soapbox podiums, come to the silent prayer vigil. Both parties are there, pro and anti, for and with, with and without, inside and outside, rich and poor, up and down, present and future. The protesters share candles from the same box and borrow zippos from each other for lighting them. Then the screaming begins. Who has the bigger candle? Bigger desire? Better rhetoric? The circles of their picket lines meld into a figure eight. Nobody notices the loop. Marching the emotional goosestep. Beer-belly riot police smoke Players and talk football. The journalists look so snappy in their trenchcoats, our legislation bookies. What shall we do with the unwanted issues of love? Don't trip on the camera cable! Don't cross the police line! Don't give up! Hold firm the tautologies! Insist on new laws for unformed bodies! Pamphlets! More Pamphlets! Say the rosary faster! We love ourselves, we love ourselves. We love ourselves too much not to

duct tape.) Your thighs like pale seaflowers slammed by whitecaps. He knelt before you with graceless and concentrated silence. I saw you begin to shake gently as though you were rooted and water gushed past your tubers underground. You bit your lip. I understand this now as your complicity with an ambiguous death, the first I witnessed. You did not call out but arched like a slow acrobat on a windshook trapeze. He exhaled, his tension dispersing. He withdrew the wire and blood ran down towards his wrist. You turned away. You finished the contract, withdrawing a ten dollar bill. He nodded in goodbye. He wiped the sweat from his forehead with the back of his hand. He disappeared through the alleyway garbage. You turned to gaze at

---

argue. We caress the cancers away. We make documentaries. We pucker up and make sucking sounds towards the unprepared womb. Thighs tremble in the stirrups. She is so beautiful. Do not scorn her. She is cold. Do not castigate. She is scared. Do not damn. She is so beautiful, but not because she is cold and scared. She is so beautiful. The air is enough. The light breeds sorrow enough. Time sorrows sorrow enough. Ambiguity is our fluorescent classroom. Somewhere somebody is watching this on tv and beating off. Live broadcast on The Abortion Channel, available through the catheter cable hookup. The metaphysical surgeons snap on their rubber gloves. A switch is thrown. The ontological suction gurgles wetly. The cameras turn. A nozzle enters. The thighs tremble and the feet contract as if in seizure. Van Gogh's irises hang on the clinic wall in reproduction. Out comes a little hand, wriggling out missed piano lessons. Out comes a tiny foot, all could've-been forest paths compressed into the one-way avenue towards Rubbermaid Mecca. Very neat, very clean. Now comes deformity. Out comes a proto-eye that will never read Humanae Vitae or Andrea Dworkin. Out comes an indeterminate organ. All heartbeats compressed into these. Sixty years, seventy years, seventy-two years collapsed into months, but who can quantify a lifespan of dreaming? Adoption? Who would want to adopt this cultural history? Womb-dreams may suffice for a lived life, says a hidden voice. Somewhere there are tears of pure formaldehyde. Somebody give that reporter a surgical mask! Get that novelist out of here! This is a sterile

the sky like Teresa of Avila watching the beginning of a rainfall on a verdant hillside while in the village below gypsy musicians strike up an ancient quadrille. Thank God your imagination healed everything, sister, or was it mine? I stuffed my entire hand down my craw to wrest loud sobs from your beatified audition. You broke your trance, pulled up your tights and followed him out into the city. I approached your dissolving altar. I knelt. I reached toward the blood and found the glowing bit of mucus that was your child. I put it to my face to smell for you, to look for the beginnings of a hand, a foot. It smelt of blood and fish and oxidizing metal and that acrid liquor I have come to know. As always, you had disappeared. I would come to

---

environment! Out comes a vertebral stringiness. Now comes death. Out comes the suspicion of brain. One wonders whether it incorporated the vacuum-sound into the end of its dream as the sleeper inserts the sound of the alarm clock into apocalyptic reverie. And now death comes again. And then it came with a whimpering flourish. And then it used to matter. And then it didn't used to matter. And now it almost matters. And now matter is replicated. And now the unnamed are glorified. Their choir sings so sweetly from our shared abattoir. Blessed autistics of grace. Marshall McLuhan incenses the shrine with tear gas from a chrome-plated canister labelled in Esperanto. Let's postulate lost talents! O God, cry the suburbanites — there goes our next Norman Rockwell! Let's estimate population curves! Apparently we are aging. Let's write tracts! Desktop publishing makes it so easy — PolemicMaker 5.1 for Windows. Let's find scriptural parallels! Let's identify the costumes of the heroine and the whore! Let's be sure of our politics! Let's wear acrylic roses in our lapels! Let's collect the translucent remains of the operation in a mason jar filled with vitriolic tears! Let's hold that jar to the light like Galileo's hunch-backed slave playing in wonderment with the first telescope!

And now, more calmly, let us rejoice in our one night stand on the planet... praying from both sides of the fence... watch the ultrasound and augur reasons for living and not living... mourn the day that kept us safe from spiritual interrogation... take these forceps and pull ourselves forward into the dark... yes, the undertakers feel cheated. Let us conjure

expect this, knowing that to approach a crystal makes its prism invisible to the naked begging eye. I dropped the wormish growth into a dumpster which was filled with rotted plaster and wooden moldings carved with cherubs that had surrounded the altar inside. At that time the diocese was renovating the cathedral to prepare for the arrival of the Pope.

Love to be with this woman on her brokenwombed journey home. Let us conjure Love for her. Not a husband. Not a father. Not a mother. Not a brother. Not a sister. Not a friend. Not a saint. Not a sinner. Not a martyr. Let us conjure Love for her. You.

26.

THIS IS THE SOURCE OF YOUR SUBLIME LAUGH-TER. I went to the sacristy and retrieved the Roman Missal. I brought it outside and opened it on the lip of the dumpster. I recited the Funeral Mass For A Young Child over the garbage, directing my voice towards the streak of blood. The dismantled cherubs listened although their plaster ears were chipped. I had trouble with the Latin pronunciation. I chose readings from Ecclesiastes and Job. I read them in the vulgar language.

27.

Who was that man, Veronica? I asked.
shhhh you said.

28.

THIS IS THE STORY OF THE DOUBLE CONSCIOUS-NESS OF CHRIST. KNOWLEDGE OF MIRRORS, WEEPING OF THE LOVE-FALL. THE SKY SPLITS AND HALF OF EVERYTHING ASCENDS BY SHIT-TING ON THE OTHER HALF. THE DOUBLE CON-SCIOUSNESS OF CHRIST PASSES ITS GIFT FROM ONE LOBE TO THE OTHER, SAD JUGGLER OF BUR-DEN AND FRUIT. THE BODY STEPS OUT OF ITSELF LIKE A TEARDROP, SALT ON THE LIPS, I WONDER WHERE I WAS BORN TO WIND UP HERE. THE BAPTIST IN A HARLEQUIN COSTUME. ONE LUNG TUMOROUS AND THE OTHER STRETCHED AGAINST AN ARIA. FERMATA. SHOWING YOUR MOTHER A SON WITH A BEAUTIFUL FACE AND A DEFORMED SPINE. THE DOUBLE CONSCIOUSNESS OF CHRIST IS A DELICATE PIECE OF COUNTER-

WEIGHT, TOO TIRED TO COLLAPSE. IT IS A CAT PAWING AT ITS MATE, FROZEN UNDER A STAIR-WELL. THE HOSPITAL CHAPLAIN AND THE HEROIN ADDICT, WHO CONFESSES TO WHOM? IT IS ONE LOVER CUTTING THE ROPE BY WHICH THE OTHER IS SUSPENDED FROM BARN RAFTERS. HAIL AND THE SUNFLOWER. THE DOUBLE CON-SCIOUSNESS OF CHRIST IS DEAF AND BLIND, YET HEARS BEAUTIFUL COLOURS. ELECTRICITY SUS-PENDED BETWEEN TWO DEAD SYNAPSES. ONE EYE FROM THE CORPSE DONATED TO A CHAR-WOMAN IN BRAZIL, THE OTHER TO AN ACCOUNTANT IN CHICAGO. PICTURES OF THE PIETA TAKEN BEFORE AND AFTER THE PSYCHOT-IC HAMMERS THE MARBLE. THE DOUBLE CON-SCIOUSNESS OF CHRIST IS A MOSQUE IN KEY WEST. THE DOUBLE CONSCIOUSNESS OF CHRIST WATCHES TELEVISION IMAGES OF APOLLO MIS-SION BOOSTER ROCKETS FALL INTO THE MEDITERRANEAN. WHAT A PIECE OF LANGUAGE IS CHRIST, WHAT WE HAVE HOLLERED HIM OUT TO BE. THE DOUBLE CONSCIOUSNESS OF CHRIST SAYS I KNOW THIS DRAMA I'VE READ THIS DRUGSTORE PAPERBACK BUT FUCKIT I'M GOING TO READ IT AGAIN, THIS TIME WITH THE EYES OF A CHILD. THE DOUBLE CONSCIOUSNESS OF CHRIST WRITES POEMS ABOUT WATCHING ITS LOVER, SOMETIMES CALLED THE WORLD, SLEEP. (psalmody of oral votive wish... hymnody of sacral cauteri-zation... grace the assembly line sodomy... as somebody else said : ordinary eternal machinery... skull skill sculling pretty pretty black chugga chugga chugga chugga rr ' t ' t' ruach ruach row)

29.

Veronica, it is overcast in the month of the dead. You told me that "to overcast" means to sew the leaves of a book together. You told me that these were the days when the world was bound between covers. You told me that sunshine destroys the overcasting and bleeds the leaves dry. You cunning linguist. O Veronica, from my window I see that the sun is coming out....

I was five. We were in the bath. The bathroom was lined with broken tiles stained by rusty water spat from leaden pipes. Your Barbie went swimming with my G.I. Joe. Barbie let her Tropical Splash bikini top slip down. Barbie straddled G.I. Joe with brute force. Joe dropped his pistol-grip Winchester in mid-hump. Sated, you turned your attention to shining the cold water nozzle with the washcloth and then squatting over it to examine your down. You washed my tiny dick so gently, like rinsing a dove found flopping in an oil slick. I pointed at your appendix scar and said

What is that? and you replied with hit-man nonchalence :

it's where they sewed me up after you came out.

I came out of there?

yes.

Did it hurt?

yes.

Did you bleed?

yes.

Did you cry?

no.

Why?

because i was chosen for your birth.

Who chose you?

god chose me.

How did you know?

i guessed.

and later you showed me your rancid appendix, shrivelled like a cannibal trophy, floating in a mayonnaise jar filled with brine. You said

look. this is your twin.

30.

I think the word for your wisdom is **deconstruction**, Veronica. The **theoretical practice** of the **postmodern mind**, which, I'm told, is characterized by **incredulity towards metanarratives**. That is, we don't believe the big stories anymore. Birth. Love. Death. All bullshit. Blank cue-sheets blowing across a false-front movie set. That is, we don't believe our lives anymore. We pretend to wound ourselves against razor-lined cages whose open doors we avoid looking for, because we're all such stubborn romantics... we can't really scald ourselves on the breath of angels... we don't believe the world anymore... we are paranoid neurotics condemned to a speech which is but a gnawing of our own turds. In order to be happy we must find our turds tasty by some remotely possible human will exerted over a cynical palate. Which is what you taught me, sister... your metaphysical cuisine... your dainty baroque placemats laid over the abbatoir lino of our dining room table.

We stood under the sanctuary lamp during one of our

many unsanctioned midnight masses* and you took me up on your shoulders so that I was eye-level to the flame and you told me to blow it out.

What?

blow it out.

What do you mean?

exactly what i said.

But it holds the Easter fire.

i said blow it out, you idiot.

But how will we replace it?

we'll make a new one.

You blow it out, Veronica.

Then you bit my thigh.

Ow, I said. Fuck.

now blow it out and watch your language.

So I blew it out, my breath circling the lampmouth. It hummed like a Coke bottle. For a moment the wick held the glow like a cigarette cherry. Then it died too, puffing a geyser of white smoke. And the Easter fire, which the Archbishop had struck with his arthritic hands in the vestibule while the last of the March hail drummed thickly outside, was gone. I was shocked. Weird child I was, worried by desecration in the age of Ozzy Osbourne. It should have all been so funny.

o don't look so fucking guilty, you said. *what makes a fire holy, little one? what was so special about that flame? that a bishop lit it with his fat little fingers? that we chanted ancient love songs to its first sparks?*

I began to cry. Still lifted on your shoulders. Crying at the windows, the blackened windows. You took out a package of wood matches. It was a yellow cardboard matchbox that said **FAMILY VALUES SAFETY MATCHES. Average 40 Contents. Made in Latvia**. You drew one out. It had a brown tip. You struck it and handed it to me.

* "All civilization consists of boys and girls playing ancient roles in forbidden theatres." — Freud

light the lamp. believe in matches. believe in the family values corporation. believe in latvia. the reeking factories. saltpetre and cordite on cracking lips. know that human beings worked in a match factory and therein was contained all human experience and they did punch the time clocks for eternity. in latvia, holy latvia! be a nationalist for a country you know nothing about. have pride. o saint voly, patron of fatty sausages! sing with me: latvia, sweet latvia our mothers and fathers died for thee. do you hear the trumpets, little one? o saint ilza, protectress against vile mongol and bestial russian! go on, light it. fire is good.

A swallow cried out as it flitted over the floodlamps outside. It sounded like a pocketwatch ground under a Doc Marten.

31.

THIS TOO IS A PREFACE. WHY IS EVERYTHING BEGINNING OVER AND OVER AGAIN, AS THOUGH WE CANNOT DECIDE WHAT TO DO WITH THE SUN? IS THERE NO THAT WILL CONSUME HISTORY? DO WE OWN NOTHING BUT DREAMS IN THIS DREAM MUSEUM? THOSE SHREDS OF WEDDING DRESS. THAT GODDAMNED SPARROW. BITS OF LUNAR DUST DANCING THROUGH THE SATELLITE BEAM, CAUSING THE MAIN CHARACTER IN SOMEONE'S FAVOURITE SITCOM TO FALL IN LOVE UNEXPECTEDLY. ALL THE SCRIPTWRITERS ARE SCRATCHING THEIR HEADS. THIS HAS BEEN WRITTEN. THIS WILL NEVER BE READ. ALL A PREFACE, A RANDOMIZED VOCALESE IN MIDWINTER, WARMING ARCTIC RESONATORS. LA LA LA LA LA LA LAAAA. BREATHE, ASCEND

ONE-HALF TONE. LA LA LA LA LA LA LAAAA
<CRACK> EMPTINESS, THINKING OF SNOW-
FORMED EVIDENCE OF OUR PASSING, DECAYING
IN APRIL. MOTIONLESS WORDS ON THE
TELEPROMPTER, ONE HOUR BEFORE BROADCAST
TIME. THE HARD DRIVE LOOKING FOR A START-
UP PROGRAM. THE PROJECTIONIST HAS PACKED
UP AND GONE TO HOLLYWOOD TO PURSUE AN
ACTING CAREER. YOU'RE THE ONLY PERSON IN
HERE, STARING AT THE SCREEN OF YOUR OWN
RETINA. YOUR LIFE IS CONTROLLED BY A TV
PRODUCER OR AD EXEC DISGUISED AS A MONK.
ALL A PREFACE. SEE GLOSSARY. INDEX. TABLE
OF. TABLEAU OF CONTEXT. INCIPIT LAMENTA-
TIO. YUP. STILL LISTING THE DRAMATIS PER-
SONAE. ROLLING THE INITIAL CREDITS.
AUTHOR, MEET YOUR CHARACTER. CHARAC-
TER, KILL YOUR AUTHOR. AUTHOR, DIE GRACE-
FULLY AS THE PLAYERS TAKE THE STAGE,
THANKING YOU FOR THE BRILLIANT LINES
YOU'VE GIVEN THEM. OPENING GALA TONIGHT,
OR ANY NIGHT. HERE COMES THE RED CARPET.
HERE COMES THE HISTORIAN TO OFFER CON-
TEXT FOR YOUR EXISTENCE. HERE COMES THE
HAGIOGRAPHER WITH SOME INTRODUCTORY
COMMENTS. DEUS IN ADIUTORIUM. IN THE
NAME OF THE FATHER, THE SON AND THE HOLY
GHOST. THE LORD BE WITH YOU. AND ALSO
WITH POO. YOUR SEATS ARE ON THE MEZZA-
NINE LEVEL, ON THE LEFT HAND SIDE. AS INDI-
CATED IN THE PROGRAM, THE PART OF THE
NARRATOR WILL BE PLAYED BY. WHEN THE
LIGHTS IN THE VESTIBULE FLASH YOU ARE
ASKED TO DOWN YOUR CHALICES AND RETURN
TO YOUR KNEELERS FOR THE SECOND HALF OF
THE PERFORMANCE. WE INVITE YOU NOW TO
STAND AND JOIN IN THE SINGING OF OUR

ENTRANCE HYMN. THE ORGANIST WILL PLAY
THE LAST EIGHT BARS OF THE PIECE FOR A
LEAD-IN. WATCH FOR THE UPBEAT. WHEN MY
ARM COMES UP LIKE THIS, TAKE A DEEP
BREATH. THIS WON'T HURT A BIT. YOU WON'T
FEEL A THING. ALL A PREFACE. THE SOUND OF
AN INSOMNIAC CLEARING HIS THROAT. AHEM
AHEM AHEM A HIM HYMEN A HYMN:

32.

o jesus o god I'm dyin' for you Veronica
you're glyphed on the walls of ol' Thessalonica
goddamn it there's pocket lint in my harmonica
It won't blow, it won't blow

[APPLAUSE]

, *

---

* Until the nineteenth century, the comma was employed in the Roman Missal to textually denote the pause that occurs during the elevation of the host at the consecration of the mass. It is believed that transubstantiation occurs during this pause.

33.

Veronica, I list your apparitions, miracles and cures on uncured vellum. I roll it and bind it with a lock of your hair and send it to Rome. The messenger drops dead in the Sistine Chapel after handing it over. The pope yawns and scratches his ass with the crook of his staff and opens the scroll. The hair transfigures and gleams. The Holy See is blinded. He staggers in latinate execration. Technicians cue the disco balls, which pop out of the genitals of frescoes. Choirboys break into a howling triumphal march to divert the cameras.

We used to play Space Invaders for hours. They lined up like the armies of angels in '50s catechism texts. We took turns sliding our lego-esque avatars along the bottom of the screen, sending up slow bolts of love into the bodies of light, right between their feelers, which opened and closed with the program of flight. We killed thousands at a time, getting better, always better, winning more and more Time in Space, winning the illusion of better and faster weapons.

34.

School was a gas, Ronnie. You paraded through columns of blackrobes like a peacock come to defame the anemic librarians of the dead. Do you remember the science fair? You described your project to me a week before Lent: *my project is called the effect of blood and urine upon the graven image.*

All the other crewcut dorks made decorative underlinings with multicoloured felt pens on gleaming white bristol boards. This made Fr. Oldgrave, the Science Priest, happy; he held his chin higher with every underlining, he puffed out his gut and stroked it with fingertips ochre from DuMaurier 100's.

You, however, wrote with a dull black wax pencil on

(Keep vigil with me, kind confessors. You passing faces in windows. Driver of a glass truck the morning after street riots. Keep vigil you barman polishing glasses under the mirror-paintings of gloveless boxers and Depression-

crinkled, greasy butcherpaper. If you were consistent in nothing else you were a stickler for formalism. ~~the presentation must mimic the subject. that's why video pinball is so stupid.~~

I have kept the science project butcherpaper:

~~purpose:~~

to investigate the effects of various bodily excretions associated with trauma and death upon an actual image of trauma and death. in this experiment, i, veronica, who am named for all true images, will examine the interaction between the real and its representations towards a more complete understanding of what it is that we believe when we insist that we believe something. my initial hypothesis is that we never really have any clue, because we are morons. i will not prove myself wrong in this, because i know that there is nothing at stake in this experiment that we haven't lost already.

materials:
4 mason jars
4 three-inch crucifixes. brass christs glued to plastic fauxwood. available from catholic truth society religious goods. bond street
2 litres of milk
2 litres of welch's grape juice
my brother's piss
my piss
pig's blood from the riverdale

slaughterhouse
lamb's blood
butcherpaper from porco fresco
meats, college street, for recording
results

method:
 the experiment will chart the pro-
posed interactions between icons and
the urines produced by grape juice and
milk and the blood of pigs and
lambs over a period of 40 days, as
this length of time has been delegated
by our tradition to be sufficient for
the creation of penitence among its
masses. i would like to think of the
images employed in this experiment
as suffering through a lent of self-
examination. we proceed as follows:
 - my brother and i commence a 24
hour fast from liquids
 - we each drink a litre of milk,
after evacuating our empty bladders
one last time, and wait for the liquid
to digest.
 - we rinse mason jars and lids
with boiling water to eliminate cont-
amination
 - at the point of urinary rupture, we
piss into one of the jars, and this
becomes sample fluid number one
 - repeat the process the following
day using grape juice as pissfuel,
labelling the two jars carefully
 - we fill the remaining two jars,
one with pig's blood, one with lamb's
blood, labelling each carefully
 - after mass on the morning of

era strippers. Keep vigil, you lady pressing a xeroxed pamphlet into my hand saying **This is for your soul** with cartoons of **buicks falling into flaming chasms at the end of the world,** accompanied

by quotes
from
~~revelation~~ in
bold face
when I was
ten years
old. Keep
vigil with
me, you
librarians
taking
gravol on
streetcars.
Keep vigil
with me you
telephone
operators
placing
reversed-
charges
calls
between
estranged

our hypothetical ash wednesday we remove the crucifixes from their packages and hold them over the open jars. we commence an appropriate prayer, and on the emphasized – men of a-men we drop the icons into their liquid dungeons at exactly the same moment, ensuring their brewing-time to be equal. we place the lids firmly on the jars

– we set the jars in south-facing windows, proceeding on the theory that each should be treated as a seedling plant. it would be foolish to keep the specimens from the sun. it would be highly unnatural. blood and urine and the signs of heaven are not meant to be hoarded away from the sun. it is only in these recent disembodied times that we hide our excretions like neurotic cats tenderfooting through victorian manor houses filled with marzipan furniture. if i had my way i would shit right here on the classroom floor and squish the turd into the carpeting with my naked toes. (incidentally, dear adjudicator, this description may now put you in mind of my project for last year, in which i planted an assortment of holy medals in seedling trays with fresh earth and fertilizer and watered them daily. as i'm sure you'll remember, they did not grow into the miraculous visions of those angels and saints they claimed to represent, just as i predicted) observations:

our observations must begin as a catalogue of the experimenters' experience. this is an investigation that puts the detectives on trial. science rarely does this. in the process, our relationships towards love and the world will be scrutinized by visions of love and the world we are not separate from this experiment precisely because we are its formulators. our white lab coats are stained with blood, piss, and hawaiian punch.

1. buying the materials:

we didn't actually buy anything. in keeping with the notion of the 'natural process', in which i firmly believe, it was essential that materials be gathered and scavenged. this experiment is about the natural decay of the garbage of love, and it is against my ethics to buy either garbage or love, yuk yuk yuk. we stole the mason jars from our mother's cupboard. we climbed the fence of the slaughterhouse yard with two milk jugs and filled them from the blood outtake spouts, one on the pig side, one on the lamb side. i will observe here that the shrieking parade of animals disappearing through the slaughterdoor made us lightheaded and giddy. we remembered the psalm that says 'yahweh does not ask for holocaust or victim' and we knew that it was crap. the next day we went to the catholic truth society with blood still on our

lovers. You Irish turf cutters in yellow rubber suits, smoking in the rain. You exiles spattered through the assholes of sociologists and carried to the rivers of sad freedoms. Keep vigil with me you overweight flower girl selling teddy bears from sex-

club to
sex-club in
the Toronto
snow,
slipping in
stilettoes
and
covering
her frostbite
with rouge.
Stay with
me, aunts
connected
to the
family tree
by catheter
tubes. Be
with me,
you grand
dame
ballroom
madwoman
of

shoes. my brother created a diversion
at the counter playing twenty questions
with the blue-haired nun behind the
cash saying

um, sister, um, how do you say the
angelus?

Well it's a special prayer to
Mary that began as a way of
praying for the crusaders in
their glorious mission of con-
quest...

right. uh, uh, what are the pope's
intentions for this week?

The Holy Father wants us to
pray for those poor unborn
babies...

o.k., right, like my twin. i'll
remember to do that. next question
what exactly is a scapular anyway, sister,
and what is it used for?

Well it's a blessed object of
devotion that comes in two
colours...

do you mean like cherry pez and
orange pez?

I suppose so, dear. Now, the
brown scapular is the badge of
the Confraternity of Carmel, in
memory of when the Blessed
Virgin appeared to St. Simon
Stock. She gave him a scapular,
promising that every one who
wore it and lived piously would
escape damnation.

what?

Damnation, dear.

oh.

Now, the blue scapular is a

devotion in honour of Our Lady's Immaculate Conception, and it requires the wearers to live a life of chastity…

what?

Chastity.

what's that?

Chastity is opposed to lust, disposing us to preserve the mind and body from everything that is impure. Chastity is purity. It is termed the angelic virtue, because it makes its practitioner resemble the angels in heaven.

how do you get chastity?

Study the angels.

oh. ok so what's yer bestselling holy medal?

Well Our Lady of Lourdes does quite well, but the Miraculous Medal of the Seven Dolours is always a favourite…

seven dollars?

No, Seven Dolours.

oh well that's very nice. now um, uh, oh, i know – who was st. rose of lima?

Well you know she lived in Peru a long time ago and burned her face with lye soap and mortified her flesh every day because she was very holy…

gee whiz sister do you mean that she whipped herself until she bled all over, even on her boobs too?

Well I don't know about that and anyway that's not terribly

Lakeshore Boulevard outside the ruined Palais Royale, let me read your liver-spot choreography and learn the twirls that keep you immaculately close to the oncoming traffic. Stay with me, Sally Ann trumpeter. Stay with me, nurses

on night
shift in the
maternity
ward,
moving
between
incubators.
Be with me,
old ladies
retrieving
eyeglasses
from plastic
handbags to
squint at
lottery
tickets.
Keep vigil
with me,
you last
black
chauffeur in
Manhattan,
let us polish

appropriate language...

holy cow sister, i mean i'm sorry,
but i'm really interested in this. like,
can you tell me, are there any mystics
left who still whip themselves, i
mean really hard like that? whaddya
think of that sister, pretty craaaaazy
huh? i wouldn't do that, no sir-
ree although i saw some women once
in a magazine pretending to whip
themselves but i don't think they were
saints...

Now young man I've just about
had enough with your...

meanwhile i stuffed four crucifixes
into my training bra. they were pack-
aged like dimestore toys, covered
with bubbles of molded plastic
attached to cardboard backings printed
on the front with cartoons of calvary
and on the back with helpful sugges-
tions for hanging. we were like those
jews in medieval mystery plays who
steal the consecrated host in order to
crucify it all over again. they hide
their sidelocks under headbandages and
whiten their tanned olive faces with
flour. they line up at the communion
rail. they hold the host in their
mouths and leave the church in
stealth. (incidentally, this observation
is now consolidating my plans for a
future experiment, which is provi-
sionally titled the effect of blood and
urine on the consecrated body of
christ. i think that once we have discovered how icons decay, we should

examine the decay of the real thing. but i will not embark upon that until i have become much more disciplined in my understanding of the sacred.)

2 preparing the samples:
the only thing that merits documentation here is that strange exuberance with which we pissed into the jars. my brother grinned with relief and hummed the ancient tune of down in adoration falling as his golden stream arced into the mouth of the jar, splashing. when he was through i squatted like a dark and weighty goddess and finished the job. we noted the differing timbres, the milkpiss being of a deeper amber brewed than the juicepiss. we were so excited by the process that we turned to each other with throbbing hearts in engorged bodies and began to kiss, standing barefoot in our spillage. later, we washed the floor with rags that had once been a shirt worn by our father.

How well I remember that day, Veronica. The holy warmth of the jars when I picked them up and held them to my chest like stillborn twins in formaldehyde. How we took them to the garage and began step number

3. waiting for decay:
we hid the jars in the garage and set them in the south facing window. our lives continued. our father slept

the ebony hood together in a single bulb garage and listen to Son House 8-tracks. Stay with me, you aestheticians planting trip-wire mines in religious icons. Be with me, paramedics on country roads working on the child

knocked off
his bike
into the
ditch by a
timber
truck. Cry
with me as
the
batteries on
your
flashlights
die out and
you lose
sight of the
gaping
aorta,
flicking
your zippos
madly over
the wound.)

through the bellringing hour one friday morning and was nearly fired. our mother was painfully quiet and read young bride magazine after washing the dinner dishes. occasionally we wondered about the crucifixes. occasionally we wandered past cemeteries and wondered about past lives. then we thought of other things. we are an easily distracted species. i examined my growing breasts in the mirror every evening. sometimes measuring my bustline with a rosary. my chest grew from 38 to 42 hail mary's during that time. i discovered that the plastic mary icon that our mother kept on top of the tv was a lovely tool for masturbation. mother caught me taking it to my room. pleased at what she thought was my new devotion, she bought me my very own when her baby bonus cheque came in the mail. my brother and i marked off the forty days on a calendar of martyrs. we became more frequent lovers. he had a number of dreams in which he was drowning.

conclusions:

the iron-dissolved nutrients, leukocytes and platelets of the blood had no visible effect upon the icons except that coagulation caused the crucifixes to stand upright. when we retrieved the blood jars, the blood had become solid, cracking on its top surface like rancid pudding. the urea, uric acid, creatinine, inorganic salts, metabolic proteins and complex pigments of our piss defaced the bronze christs, marring the polished surface with pocks not unlike syphilis scars. it softened the plastic of the crucifixes. there was no notable difference between the milkpiss and juicepiss although i imagine that the milkpiss, being darker, incurred more damage upon the icon on the molecular level, the effects of which would have to be seen by microscope, but this is assuming that i give a shit about that kind of detail. the point is that a brother and a sister pissed on the icons that governed their imaginations from the cradle. then we called it science. and we learned something. don't ask me what. go do it yourself.

acknowlegements:
i'd like to thank the riverdale slaughterhouse and the catholic truth society. my apologies to the nun who sacrificed her 1930's girl's boarding school knowledge for the sake of low comedy. i'd especially like to thank my brother for sharing this adventure in faith with me. and i'd like to thank you, dear reader and adjudicator, for witnessing it all.

And now I fold it up, Veronica, the same butcherpaper that was wrenched from your hands by Father Oldgrave on the day of the presentation... Do you remember? You stood in front of the class and took the mason jars out of the milkcrate we had carried giggling and nervous through the March slush. You placed them in a line across the front of the desk, cleared your throat, rustled the butcherpaper, and began to read.

title: the effect of blood and wine on the graven image

Father Oldgrave rose from his dozing posture in the back of the classroom. Kids looked up from meditations on boredom and guilt. I took a breath and wanted to run.

purpose:

veronica: to investigate the effects of various bodily excretions associated with trauma and death upon an actual image of trauma and death FATHER OLDGRAVE: That will be enough, young lady. Remove those jars from sight. *veronica: in this experiment. i, veronica, who am named for all true images,* FATHER OLDGRAVE: Veronica sit down. *veronica: will examine the interaction between the real and its representations towards a more complete understanding* FATHER OLDGRAVE: In the name of Christ, I'll *veronica: of what it is that we believe when we insist that we believe something.* FATHER OLDGRAVE: see to it that *veronica: my initial hypothesis is that we never really have any clue,* FATHER OLDGRAVE: your blasphemy is [Narrator: Father begins to walk up the aisle, leaning into his fury. O Veronica please stop reading] *veronica: because we're morons. i will not prove myself wrong in this,* Students (the boys): Oooooh, she's gonna get it. Too cool. *veronica: so i proceed just for the fun of it, knowing that there is nothing at stake in this experiment that we haven't lost.* Students (the girls): Aaaaaaaah no, her hair, your beautiful raven hair, o priestess! *veronica: already.* [Narrator (stage whisper): Where's my prompter? Cue trap door!] FATHER OLDGRAVE (seizing your hair, O sister please desist): Veronica, how dare you. *veronica: fuck off you iconolater for your popish images have come to naught* FATHER OLDGRAVE: Veronica how dare *veronica: fuck* FATHER OLDGRAVE: you *veronica: you.* FATHER OLDGRAVE: Veronica how dare *veronica: fuck you.* FATHER OLD-

GRAVE: Veronica how veronica: *fuck you*, FATHER OLDGRAVE: Veron veronica: *fuck you* FATHER OLDGRAVE: ica veronica: FATHER OLDGRAVE: Vero veronica: *fu* FATHER OLDGRAVE: n veronica: *ck* FATHER OLDGRAVE: i veronica: *y* FATHER OLDGRAVE: c veronica: *ou* FATHER OLDGRAVE: a

[Cut to Carole Burnett credits, cartoon of Ms. Burnett replaced by Robert Crumb animation of dominatrix sodomizing flabby Basilian with strap-on. Fade to canned laughter.]

35.

Veronica, I've just heard that Father Oldgrave was killed in a hunting accident. The greasy pederast was shot by a Jesuit aiming at a warthog. If I can get myself out of bed today I'll go to the autopsy and gloat over his black heart.

36.

Veronica, let us return to our Easter turkey bones in the compost heap. Those worms have been very busy indeed. — How I too long for vocation!

We took the same bus driven by the same bus driver up to the same place. Desiccation sang slow dripping notes to curl up the ends of the summer. You craned your neck to listen for the cicadas.

The fishnet stocking had dissolved, leaving the bones to gleam like the teeth of bog people. We pulled them out of the mound in the humid dusk. They came away clean.

We got them home and laid them out on our bedroom floor. We consulted an anatomy text for fowl and numbered and labelled each bone. We arranged them into the correct pattern on the carpet. You varnished each bone with Barbie Beauty Nail Polish. Then we affixed each joint with airplane glue. Soon we had a fully assembled turkey skeleton. You gave it another coat of nail polish.

You looked at it and said *so much for the resurrection of the body.*

Then we played more Space Invaders, although with a new rule: you had to say "I love Satan" every time an Invader splatted.

37.

Veronica, did you know that all the widows have lit their candles in our old cathedral and each flame throws your silhouette against the stone wall? They think they are mourning for themselves but the names they wail signify you, their daughter. They have no idea how you will appear. As one of our brightest scholars says, "The terms and methods in which prayers are answered are as remote to most worshippers who light candles before images as is the theory of electricity to most of us when we switch on the light."* — Their performance is immaculate.

Now it's angelus time. A fat lady with short brown hair gone stringy and black with humility grease is leading the prayer from the marble pulpit. She's wearing a support girdle under a boxy dress of popsicle blue colour. A thick-beaded gold-colour chain hangs from the arms of her cataract glasses. Nasal intonation and pursed lips make it sound like she's talking to herself while having a stringy bowel movement in a grain silo. Her sisters and brothers in prayer stare at their hands or at the windows and make their responses like sci-fi extras. The light wraps and unwraps itself in frayed grey bandaging that smells of wet porphyry and old sage.

I'm as tired as anyone here. The shadows of birds swoop

---

* Many churches have installed new electric votive lights for their customers' praying convenience. You can now deposit the correct change into the slot and press a button at the base of the candle/lightbulb of your choice. This is the video slot-machine of devotion — if you choose the right lightbulb, crystal coins of beneficence will gush out of the slot and land in the lap of your intention. The cutest aspect of the system is that when the candles are all lit, the machine will arbitrarily extinguish one upon the insertion of more coins, to free up a lightbulb for the new customer. The implication is, of course, that God can only care about a specific number of intentions at any one time — in this case, the number of lightbulbs available for lighting. It's not such a harsh thought, really. After all, isn't the holiest desire the one that escapes attention, or the one that is completely erased for another to take its place?

past the clerestory like the stetsons of old men throwing shadows across a pornhouse screen as they look for their seats. The fat lady recites and the people follow on cue. Her amplified voice and their group moanings twine in the air, reminding me of the time when I was a kid and I went with an american cousin of mine to his farm and just for kicks we pounced on the two farm dogs in mid-coition and tied them together around the bellies with wheat baling straps. They squirmed, first angrily, then languidly in their bonds for about 20 minutes and then they stopped, panting exhaustedly, and licked each other's faces with that beautiful empathy so foreign to us.

I fell asleep in the pew with my head on my ragged copy of de Sade and a hymnbook with a broken spine.

Someone rattled a rosary by my head. I woke up and left, walking out past some guy washing his cock in the lavabo.

38.

The tabernacle looks like a huge, gold-plated espresso maker. Young families process to the communion rails, bathed in the stale light of refrigerators. They look like actors in channel 10 productions about sharing and loving and having regular medical checkups. The organist has drawn the tremulant stop.*

---

* "Tremulant" — a mechanical device, dating from the 16th century, which causes an undulating effect in the sound by disturbing the wind. The external type (tremblant à vent perdu) accomplishes this by allowing intermittent puffs of wind to escape; the internal type by means of a hinged flap that floats up and down inside the wind-trunk. In early English organs the tremulant was known as the "shaking stop." The sound is most commonly associated with Hammond B-12s rippling gelatinous haloes around the skulls of Bela Lugosi and Boris Karloff. Cf. also "The Shadow". The effect, used for approximating the unevenness of the human voice, can also be accomplished by assigning two pipes to a single note, and slightly untuning one of them, so that the overtones ripple in disagreement. This explains the wavering of my discourse, sweet one. My twin voices of joy and sorrow have been misaligned by the Organ Tuner.

After communion, the priest invites everyone to pray silently for all victims of abortion. The silence is interrupted by a baby who screeches and then chokes on its puke. The cries trail away as the mortified mother carries it down the centre aisle, her nylons swishing like fronds of palm leaves.

Later, an old woman comes in today and tries to make the statue of Jesus hold a bouquet of flowers. She is enraged when the ceramic hand doesn't close around the stems. She tears up a few missals and prayer cards and then whispers   Bill?   Bill?   to the windows.

39.

There is nothing we can say to the nineteenth century that wouldn't break its heart. This is sad, for I am nostalgic for the rationalist sensibility, wherever it is (still chewing the cud of a Perfect Universe in a movie set designed by Merchant & Ivory, most likely). I love the Old Catholic Mind... dignified in the village squares... fond of the merry sound of horses on cobblestones... always polite to gartered maids bending pertly to take out the chamber pots... soothed by dusks of camarine... nodding through funeral sermons with appropriate gravity... rightly suspicious of jesuits and monks... generally kind towards its mistresses... ah, the age of rosewood walking sticks... Who would want to assault this precious disposition from the postmodern fortress? Those who live in glass houses shouldn't drink the Windex. Let me therefore soften all frilly coffin pillows by exclaiming, with the help of an 1861 edition of the Stations of the Cross, the Prayer for the Sixth Station, a pious ejaculation of the Soul to her Crucified Redeemer:

✠ My Suffering Jesus, imprint, I beseech thee, on my soul, thy bitter torments, as thou didst impress thy sacred countenance on the towel by which the pious Veronica wiped thy face, besmeared with blood and spittle.
— (Pause and reflect upon your iniquities)

Like the time when we touched each other in the change-room of the gym in the parish hall, leaning on our elbows sixty-ninewise, naked, tenderly quivering on the white tiles, soft huffapuffs rising to the open ground-level window grown over by scrubgrass. We heard a grunt. We looked up and saw the face of our father at this same window regarding us with lust, kneeling in the dirt with his overalls down. He lept up and fled, running bow-legged and pulling up his pants. Veronica asked *i wonder if he came.* We scampered outside to search in the wallbottom muck for our gleaming half-siblings. We found nothing but waterbloated cigarette filters, stinking bootes, mucke combes, ragged rochettes, rotten girdles, ply'd purses, oh henry! wrappers, great bullock hornes, lockes of heere, a yellowing and cracked dog turd, filthy ragges, gobbettes of wodde, and a streetcar ticket valid for a day years before, when our father was younger, when he smiled more, when he took our whole family on trips to the countryside, which I remember as being vast, before those goddamned wholesale warehouses and industrial parks broke out like cubist warts... yeah, there we are now, back in the K-car of nightmares... driving, just driving... why does it seem impossible to kill yourself deliberately on the 401... you always end up stopping at a donut shop and walking in... watch your warped face grow a beard of ash in the tinfoil ashtray... rigs barrel past the grimy window, empty as deadcarts on the way back to the cold-rooms of banks... beside you a fat cop eats four crullers dunked in triple-creamed coffee while he reads Hustler... the waitress says quietly into the phone   I'm sick of this shit Matthew when are you gonna   change?   , lighting one cigarette off the last and another one off that one then she hangs up and wipes the counter with a brown j-cloth... and somehow you make your coffee last until morning...

40.

Day trip to Elora Gorge, autumn of 1977.
   Mom was telling us about the fallen leaves. *Maybe you can collect some and put them into a book. Once I made a book with birchbark covers, three-holed onionskin, bound with string, a leaf glued to every page, its name underneath in crayon. I'll show you how.*
   She's at ease in the passenger seat, shoes off and her shins under the air vent, breathing fully, out of the city, all desperate words torn away in the slipstream. Our father just drives, a passenger of his own oblivion, a vague and pleasant worry of falling asleep at the wheel, eyes catching

on the glyphs of treetops, then soothed by the belling of the road, his mind empty and open as the tires dub their hum over the slo-mo still life. Highway stripes as unreadable subtitles in a film without dialogue. He's hung over. A rosary hangs from the rear-view mirror; its crucifix banks with the curves.

The canary sun moves across an iron ore outcrop. The radio fades to static. Our father turns the dial from left to right. He finds nothing but a recorded weather report on a state channel, wind directions, warnings for fishermen.

You never ask Are we there yet? anymore: now you know the road always begins and ends in sleep. Even now you are dreaming. And you know that for dreaming travellers, the crash into the schist has always already happened, the beautiful sight none but the hawk sees, the metal twisting into the body like earth guided by furrowing rain.

Late insects swirl for last blood through rows of crimson harvest. These places are the Beyond. Glass insulators on the crosses of telephone poles glint red in the sky. No one phoning home today. The robins sleep in electromagnetic suspension.

We pass through a town. Our mother notices an antique shop, its windows strung with a dead woman's jewellery. If we had stopped there, you would have seen her ivory cameos, cutglass broaches. Stacks of brittle parlour music on the stand of a gutted piano.

We sit quietly in the back seat. Dad's empties at our feet. You play counting games with the passing hydro poles, measuring space, measuring time, mapping while in the map, one compass point piercing the memory lobe, the other piercing Broca's area. Mom says to Dad Don't drink another one in the car, o.k. please, hon?

Passing a chain of vacant fields now, one where weeds fondle the ruins of a fairground. In its grass-worn hub rises the skeletal piping of a circus tent, shreds of blue and yellow-striped vinyl dangling from the crossbar, the wires sloping upwards to the centre pole. A rusted slide. A carousel like a b-movie space ship, its metal canopy collapsed, pierced by poles that skewer horses of painted wood at obscene angles. If Dad had stopped the car, pulled by some ruined magnetism, you might have seen the glass eyes of the horses scattered in a nimbus around the scrap disk, you might have seen bottles of JD lying empty under the empty awning of the ruined concession standing empty, you might have seen a dog licking at the calcified fat charred to the hamburger grill. We would have stood there like the last tableau of a Frank Capra drama, our Jimmy Stewart Dad squeezing out a glycerine tear to lubricate our oblique sense of familial vertigo... and there's mom, soft-focussed, unreal as she ever was... the crows perching on the telephone wires like rain-blotted neums in gregorian manuscripts.

We reach the outskirts of a small town called Elora, swirling the dust on unmarked dirt roads, winding through fir trees and sliding on the autumn rain washboard. The world listening and oblivious. The pine trees bristled against the sky as though left by a silhouette artist scattering waste-slivers of black.

Our father cuts the engine with the front bumper against a low wooden railing on a precipice. You open your door, jump to the ground, and run to the edge. The gorge unfolds around you in a palette of cadmium reds and yellows. Our father puts an arm around our mother. Two-hundred-foot deciduous trees look like garden flowers from your incredible height. We all stare down into abandoned nests. The river is so far down you can see whitewater but you can't see it move. *See what I mean about the leaves?* our father asks as he takes your hand and you walk towards the wooden steps. He hands you a paper bag from his jacket pocket, saying *This is to collect the things you want.*

Our mother has taken off her shoes again, our father carries his jacket over his shoulder. He totters a bit. You jump from step to step, losing count somewhere, trying to guess where to start again, giving up. Pine cones and chestnuts underfoot. How do you decide which is the perfect one to take, which one would look best on your night table or your desk when the book under your fingers defocuses in boredom? Which stone is magical? (Which saint is the one you will model your life on? Which martyr getting her legs torn apart by horses?)

On the igneous rockfaces friezed by twisting roots from rows of trees on an overhead ledge, your mother points to fossils of the drowned creatures. In descent they become alien, family and fossil; the vertebrae shorten, become crab-like, like moving backwards from sentences to pictograms or letter fonts to Zapf Dingbats:

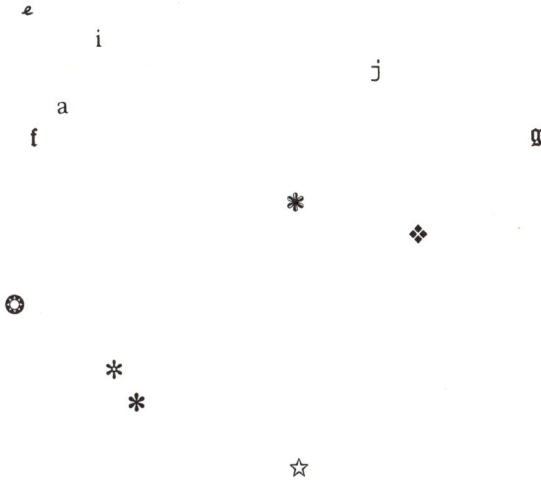

e

    i

                j

  a

f   𝖌

            ❋

                 ❖

○

    ✳

     ✳

          ☆

If grandpa had drowned here, you ask, would we see his skeleton in the rock? *Maybe, maybe,* Mom answers, remembering the face of her father, liver-spotted, his spine collapsing under the weight of alcohol and depression, how his rib cage cracked after the fourth explosion of his heart. (Nicotine floating through corroded birdcages.)

Leaves everywhere, as they have fallen. Designed or not. Can random be perfect? Can it be beautiful if unplanned? Can it be ugly?

Dad lights a smoke. The sun grows cold. Certain leaves catch your eye like Arabic in a King James Bible. You pick them up, hold them against the light, living windows veining a web of shards. Your paper bag becomes thick with leaves. Why do they change colour, dad? you ask. *The green stuff eats the sun*, good old monotone Dad, helpful as ever, *and when the sun starts to go away, the green stuff leaves too, and goes back into the ground.* (He wants a drink. He is impatient with the pastoral, like any good Yahwist. It's all desert if you look close enough. He only went for the drive.) You think of what they say in school about the soul being the part of you that lets you hear God, maybe hearing is like eating, about how God takes the soul from your body when God wants you to come. How death means that the body falls out of its soul-tree and cracks its skull against the ground, and another child comes along, picks up your corpse and holds it to the light, carries it home to press dry in a book.

By the riverbed you and I take off our shoes and socks and wade into the rushing water. You clutch my hand. We move slowly, sounding the depth with small feet. Our Father stands on the shore upstream, skipping flat stones into a calm stretch above gentle rapids. You tell me you have to pee. I look around for privacy, undo the buckle on your shorts. I hold your tiny penis — such a begging white bird! — pointing downstream, and the urine brings bubbles up on the surface trailing away. I zip you up. We continue to wade, deeper. — A trout leaps like mercury splashing from a broken compass. — You see a piece of wood cleaving a bare rock. It's a knotted root. You reach for it to steady yourself as you pull against my grasp. It snaps away in your hand, and you slip, and I pull you up out of the rapid in reflex. You cling to me, gagging, your eyes bleared with water. I carry you back because you are terrified. — I've had a vision of your spine as a fossil.

On the drive home the sun sank like a lead sinker to the bottom of a black lake, the hook lodging in rubber. Some weeks later you opened your bag of leaves. They were worm eaten, but their crimson was sweet, vampiric.

41.

In the possible geography of our happiness, the buildings will yet decay. Mortar will not stop its crumbling weep. Hinges on lockets will rust. Breath will be painful, and on.

Let's stand back and watch things be repaired or neglected. Haul sandbags. Watch the river. Watch the red ants breed, oblivious to the drowning.

In the possible geography of our happiness, we will use the verses of improbable religions to talk about the sadness of tectonic shift, highway systems of the deep south, reasons for staying around. The blue pillars. The salt in the cupboard. Stock footage of light-changes. Bottles empty and full. Objects of preparation. Stage dressing. Invitations and offerings. Improvised sacraments. Refugees here. Let's replaster the ceiling. We are not free.

42.

Our parents took their honeymoon in Niagara Falls. They really liked Marineland™. Dad got pissed in the heart-shaped Jacuzzi. He probably belted her and then got all sorry and helped her clean up her bloody lip with the Cupid-embroidered towels. In the morning she snuck the towels out in a Liquor Store bag. Everybody's fine.

Here is a picture of our father at Marineland, feeding dolphins who leap up from their chlorinated prisons. The splashing water is cold on his hand and forearm. He smiles at our mother, whose camera lens eye I peer through now. Because she was laughing in that moment, the picture is unfocused; so it is with delight and seizures.

In Israel, the parents of autistic children bring them to the beaches of Ras Muhammad on the Red Sea to play with the dolphins. Without fail, the dolphins heal them. Violent boys smile like bodhisattvas. Eleven-year-old girls who have never spoken use their voices for the first time to imitate little dolphin squeaks and whistles. Soon they are reciting the Psalms in perfect Hebrew. They gaze into the glassy eyes and giggle when the smooth blue heads brush against their waists. — These are animals that smile. — A seventy-two-year-old Birkenau survivor who had refused to open his eyes for twenty-eight years touched the dorsal fin of a young calf. He opened his eyes.

I pray to these dolphins with this litany: Heal this picture. Heal this sentence. Heal this silence between the picture and the sentence. Heal this silence between the picture and the silence. Heal this silence between the sentence and the silence. Heal this silence between the silence and the silence.

43.

Here is a picture of our father's mother receiving communion in her vinyl La-Z-Boy recliner. The priest bends over her walker. A crumb falls on her unfinished crossword. (Question: what's a five-letter word for "body"? Answer: D-E-A-T-H.). She used a magnifying glass for her crosswords. Once we stole it to scorch ants on the sidewalk.

Our grandmother had had so many children she couldn't walk. Splayed out in birthing 13 times. This was not violence in those days. It was a matter of emulating Henry Ford. Her five daughters grew up to be nurses and beaten housewives, and her sons became civil engineers and drunks. Dad was the only one to follow his vocation. They all went to mass. The ghosts of the three stillbirths hovered in the living room, telling Grandma what tv show to watch.

I remember falling into sleep against Grandma's shrivelled dug. A polyester blanket around my legs. Lawrence Welk bounced through Christmas garlands of plastic lillies on a 24-inch GE b&w. Grandma's broken voice sung along. There was a picture of the pope on the wall opposite the tv and I could watch the commercials in its glass. — I woke up when a wind ripped in from Lake Ontario and tore the antenna from the roof. Mr. Welk sputtered. Grandpa climbed up on the roof to fix the wiring. He slipped and fell past the window into the ice-sheathed snow. He went back to work on Boxing Day, pawing the wheel of the garbage truck with a cast on his right arm.

Sister, when you were absent, I learned my metaphysics from pacemakers, dentures, walkers, wheelchairs, and all small tools of simple crippled quietude. Whenever I'm in Montreal I go to L'Oratoire Ste-Joseph and count the crutches. They are signs for the subtle defeats of love.

If Grampa was still alive, I'd probably keep quiet at his nigger jokes and fag jokes and his nigger-faggot jokes.

I miss our grandparents and their Fifties Catholic Bungalow. They were so beautiful. I am hungry for this memory, this hour, holding its time to the light against the oncoming projections of ruder forms.

44.

While Our Father was the bellringer and changer of burnt-out votive candles, while he polished the heads of brass bolts in the cathedral front doors made large enough for cardinals to ride in on horseback, while he scraped guano off the tongues of gargoyles, while he swept confetti out of the vestibule, while he picked wax out of the carpet like plucking gravel out of roadburn, while he scrubbed the altar canopy clean of incense soot, while he polished the patens and chalices with blackened rags, while he removed the robin's nests from the mouths of the largest organ pipes, our mother was mute. She nursed a SILENCE as though she thought that if she spoke, small and lovable things would die at every word. Besides being the church maid and rectory laundress, she was an artisan of ceramics and glass. She was hired by the cathedral to rework the cracked rose window over the choir loft. She matched the old colours to the new, she cut replacement pieces for the petals of mystical flowers and the eyes of saints. She leaded and soldered them into place while standing on a ladder that ascended from the organ chamber. She hummed Ave Maris Stella to herself. She had a voice like tiny shards of alabaster jingling in a dixie cup. The job took ten years.

While Our Father drank and swaggered and barfed, our mother slowly turned the cathedral into an immense lantern reversed by the implacable outer light.

45.

If the woman is ill and her seizure seizes her time and again at nightfall, if she throws off her cloth time and again: seizure by an incubus.
— Babylonian Diagnostic Handbook

Can we say for sure that our mothers consented to anything?

Our Father was an ambiguous man. I suppose he loved mom in his own way but so what.

I have little evidence for Mom's unhappiness, except that my life would make more sense in the face of a Mother's Hidden and Inexplicable Sorrow. One has to have good lines to feed psychotherapists, lines they can filofax and cross-reference.

They wanted children because Nature and Reason and Tradition made them want children. I imagine that they paused in front of mirrors, trading features over the glass surface. This is how our faces were imagined. Then they touched, and the house fell in half, as a fruit will expose seed. They fell away from each other to ride the spring ebb. They were briefly fulfilled, knowing nothing of what was to come. The first insects of the season hatched over bog and marsh. How's that for a repressed and hazy description of fucking?

I am not a woman. But I can imagine the vacuum left by a man withdrawing. How death will slip out from between the sheets. Damp things turning cold. Violets weeping in milk bottles, the wallpaper eschering with possible destinies.

There is a netherland in the fallopian halfway between dream and nightmare. I was conceived on March 19, 1971. The windows filmed over. Our mother woke up kicking and moaning, throwing back her cloth. The weight pressing her chest and splaying her limbs was not her husband, but she was married to it, a sister.

The air convulsed over their bed. Hummingbirds slept in the knots of ancient oaks.

46.

Veronica, they always wanted another daughter after you. Had you wanted a sister? Is this why I became your Leslie Caron, your Natalie Wood, your Marianne Faithfull, your Traci Lords?

47.

I pray. The way you witness yourself from other eyes, blind winter barriers. The way you have made nothing of history, the way of collapse. The way possibilities are eliminated... nova, quiet and invisible... the way the pigeons in the soffits surrender to the homemade nets of the starving... bell curves of gravity and probable grace... the necrophilia that gives life... your eyes in my mouth... the imperfections of the body in the cesarean morning... the vaccination scar... the naked infusion... respite such an inaudible prophecy... suckling the blemish... receiving the penetrating accident... how everything will be vaporized and this will mean nothing... a cure for everything... a blue-sky assurance...

48.

Mother Glazing: a naturalist cipher*

Nothing is transparent. Mother's voice, as florescent as an incubator. Sunday evening in late November, she bends over the light table, cutting stained glass for the rose window. Scoring and breaking, holding the fragments up to the twilight of the ground level window, circling them with copper foil, oxidizing the edges with acid.

She is the mother of a great unity, happy in the body, unaware of the body, the body is glass.

The frost warning from the television in the next room, the loosened windows, the soldering iron hissing in its support, the smell of flux and basement mold, gentle nausea and quiet fatigue. Things are lit from underneath for labourers and saints.

Look. Look here. She's holding the glass up to your eyes. *See that? What matters is the light that's left after the passage.* She tells you that sunlight contains every colour, that the glass catches every colour except the one by which we call it. Blue glass is glass that cannot trap blue. You are eight years old.

She once told you that glass was made from melted sand, and you imagined a great fire making every surface on earth clear, every layer of rock now a shore of windows, your eyes probing the sea bottom. There are caverns, air pockets, your lungs wrapped in the gossamer sheet of your skin.

Once she took you to the museum to watch Buddhist monks create mandalas of coloured sand on the marble floor. You remembered rose windows in a book, and you imagine setting the sand windows into their vertical frames, and seeing all the glass scattering its grains with the wind, fearful and dangerous, just as the monks destroy the pattern after the final prayer, after the final light is let in and the walls murmur of stillness.

---

*Professor Warburg of the University of Berlin showed in 1930 that slices of brain tissue can survive for many hours in vitro, given the necessary ions, glucose and oxygen.

Sand. Heat. The desert is a glass factory, you decide, and those who live there must be glassblowers. You remember television images of bedouins, and imagine their endless work of somehow making the desert transluscent in the absence of water. You see one, middle-aged, sitting in a white tent with one corner pulled back, guiding the sun through a magnifying glass he holds over a pestle full of sand. You understand that this is how we are made to see, that the sand is melted, the glass flows from one world to the next, always with a falling motion before your eyes, always seductive as television. But who made the magnifying glass? Where does it begin, with what trick of mirrors, what application of light? What happens during a sandstorm?

She tells you that metal oxides are stirred into the melted sand to colour it. Selenium and gold make red, yellow and pink, and these are the most expensive glasses. Cobalt makes blue. Sulphur makes amber. Our mother has thousands of samples of glass, organized into families of colour, thickness, and texture, bound as pages in wooden frames, held together by brass hinges on the left-hand side. These are the first books of your childhood, layer of glass upon layer of glass, a game of blurred vision, unreadable except when separated, uninteresting except when opaque. Pages that colour your small hand. You experiment with what these two or three pages look like if they are overlaid, the opalescent with the antique with the granite-back, deliberately blurring the syntax. In the middle of these books the colour of the pages is an indeterminate black, like a stone containing many stones, all surfaces polished to a bright reflection. Your face in every one, or you imagine seeing flowers.

You are eight years old, and you feel you have no words for these things. You wait for the time when you do, you make up your mind not to speak until then. Your fractured cosmology a greenhouse for plasma. Your young mind, constantly adjusting the aperture.

Our Mother tells you the story about your great-aunt, a Felician nun who was put in charge of the physical upkeep of her order's motherhouse. *She kept the walls and icons painted, the tiles buffed and in good repair, the oak pews and kneelers varnished, the windows clean and tight, and the grounds healthy and green. Once a week, she would drive the convent pickup five miles into town for supplies — tools, hardware, paint, insulation, soil, fertilizer.* — An androgene... a genealogical cipher. — *Every few years she would build new shelving for the growing library.* The building is clean, quiet, and reverberant, like a hospital *early in the morning, At Christmas they would play Connie Francis Sings Our Favourite Carols in the reading room,* the ancient furnace clanging away in the basement.

In the year of her retirement, the order decided to build a new chapel, and she offered to spend her extra time making the windows. *She went to the recycling plant in Waterhaven every other week to collect pop bottles, wine bottles, beer bottles. Bringing them back, storing them in the gardening shed.* When she was ready to begin, it was early February, and she asked two of the altar boys who served on Sunday morning to help her carry the ceramics kiln from the workshop out to the clapboard shed. *She had them haul a flat stone, about 150 pounds, up out of the pond in the pasture and lay it on the rough floor next to the kiln.* — You imagine that she thanked them with holy cards and stale candy.

She would work from matins until high mass, placing the bottles, three at a time, in a large canvas bag, which she would hammer against the smooth pond rock. She emptied the bag into an iron jug which she would push into the heated kiln. Burning dregs of beer and wine, the kiln sputtering violently as the April downpour leaked through the pitch, drops of water instantly disappearing on the wrought iron surface. *When the splinters had melted, she would pour the glowing liquid out onto the stone and wait until it cooled into a sheet of textured glass with swirling colours, bearing the rough of the rock on its underside like the pores of your skin.* Our mother is telling you about the windows made from bottles, and you imagine the chapel itself as a bottle, held up to the rural light by a benevolent hand, containing things to be poured out, things to be spilled, the need to be transparent, the possibility of breaking, storylike, at any time.

(You can no longer distinguish your thoughts from *our mother's voice.*)

Years after the chapel was finished and the window panels were installed, *they found your great-aunt one morning in a confessional stall*, where she had taken to hiding in the last few months of her illness. She'd stopped eating and shivered violently when praying the rosary. *She was already cold. Still kneeling.* The nurses in the infirmary had been at a loss as to how to keep her in her bed, to comfort her when she called out, to Joseph, to Mary, to God, to Judas, and to Miguel, the gardener. She was given morphine. Fed and drained through tubes. Then she saw a very small light on the chapel altar, like a christmas tree bulb taped to a wheelchair.

The sisters commenced the funeral preparations. The night before the service, the chapel was robbed by city boys, looking for chalices, censers, candlesticks and wine. They broke through the lowest of the beer-bottle windows.

In the morning, the funeral-goers came into the chapel, seeing one side littered with shattered glass, and the town's only detective working at the gaping window, powdering jagged shards for fingerprints. *The only sounds heard were those of the detective's shoes on the crushed particulate, as he walked from the window to the sanctuary, making chalk marks on the floor and on the pews.* He was still working when the coffin was wheeled out by distant cousins, alcoholics and factory workers, awkward, in church for the first time in years. A piper marched the coffin all the way out to the hearse at the curb, while the children of the convent orphanage stood with their faces against the fence of the schoolyard, resting their chins on the diamond-shaped chainlinks, watching, omniscient. And the detective, still working under the window frame as it yawned in the early March air.

You imagine being able to avoid the funeral procession, the grieving family and the beneficent nuns, some crying, some clucking, by climbing out of that frame, unnoticed, your hands perfectly gloved, running across the pasture, chasing sense, the lengthening shadow of the tired man you will be, to the pond, to sit alone on the glassworking stone. You own this field... its light... Queen Anne's Lace... cow shit... anthills... moth wings...

You learned early that you can't draw a window except by drawing what is reflected in it, or by drawing what lies beyond it, carefully cropping it to fit the frame. The frame is a missing page in a book. The frame is a hole in your body.

Our mother tells you the fittings that hold the pieces of glass are made from lead, *the same stuff that's in your pencil,* what makes your writing visible. You imagine the lines of every pencil drawing you ever made holding pieces of glass, that the page itself is perfect glass, white being all colours, black script the absence of light, your strokes rearranging what's already there. You think of letters that close on themselves like windowframes. A. D. g. O. P. Q. R. Letters that exist because you see through them, and are seen through only because you have written them.

You ask our mother why she doesn't paint on the glass, as in the churches you know from another century, renaissance faces and symmetrical musculature visible through accretions of factory grime and diesel smoke, set into walls stained with the residue of burning votive candles, great fading arches covered with carbon-paper black.

When there is no outer light, these old windows in these old churches become canvases, offering stories to refugees and shift workers. Our mother's windows, unpainted, cease to narrate at dusk. They empty themselves for sleep and the new eyes it brings, which aren't made for continuity, or even time. *You must let the material do the work* she says. Her hair drapes over the light table. *You must allow the glass to speak, even at night. You are less important than you think.*

In Tudor England, it was the practice of the royalty to exact tax based on the size of a subject's windows. The "window tax" effectively allotted a percentage of the capital gains of *what was seen* by the populace to the coffers of the monarch. Many citizens bricked up their windows in favour of food money. They filled their stomachs and saw very little.

You place your small hand on the glowing table, and you can almost make out the bones, imagining what a lovely thing blood is, imagining the names of the metals that give you your colours, imagining swimming in your own thin body, imagining that our mother is a scientist, and yourself, conceived as a hybrid of translucence and a particular agent of crystallization, among the vials and petri dishes, their beautiful colours.

And those moments at mid-afternoon, when the other kids are in the yard, and you are in the 50's chapel that you always seem to remember first when you think of school, staring at the cold sun through the blood-glass at the feet of Salome, knowing there is a swath of red across your face. — You look down. It has spilt onto your arms as well.

49.

Mirrors
Once there was a very important argument among men of great holiness and learning concerning the letter "i". It was the fourth century. There were heads rotting on the Via Appia. Some heads were Christian heads. Some heads were Jewish heads. Some heads were Franco-Norman heads. Some heads were Greek heads. The heads talked calmly to each other in their new-found shared language like they were standing cheerfully in welfare lines. The blackened eyes watched everything. The heads of men flirted with the heads of women. The abundance of horseflies surrounding these heads gave artists the inspiration for the nimbus. Grappa was the favoured drink of executioners. Lepers were given sticks to beat together in warning. For some reason, the christians were gaining confidence. They were having strange but happy dreams of printing presses and evangelical satellites. Their children played stickball with femurs and hardened turds found in the catacombs, prefiguring depression-era scenes in North American cities. The children scratched images of fish into the underground walls. Historians say that the catacombs were never used

for holding mass during the persecutions of Diocletian but I believe that they were, for no other reason than aesthetic fancy. Mass should always be held underground. Daylight is an aberration to the holy cannibal.

In Nicaea, scholarly delegations arrived, drawn by teams of farting horses. The argument began over the letter "i".

The Greek word *homoousian* is used to describe the relationship between Jesus the Son and God the Father as being of the *same substance*. The word *homoiousian* describes this relationship in the terms of *like substance*. Note how the "i" injects the notion of s i m u l a t i o n into the term. Note how the "i" subjects the holy ding an sich to the epistemological carnie wheel of r e l a t i v i t y . , I = not the same. Note how this same letter, is used to denote the First Person Singular in our famous and quite economically successful language. So, everybody argued about which word to use in their little games. The bishops argued. The Franciscans argued. I don't know who argued what. It was extremely important to believers whether they were eating God or something like God at their eucharistic barbecues. I imagine that the monks argued against the "I", because monks are cooler than bishops.

One night Veronica and I stole the devotional triptych from the side chapel because she wanted to show me how to bury my image, my "I", in innumerable false replicas. The triptych was an image of the Trinity, the centre panel featuring the triangle eye embedded in its nest of swirling clouds and serenaded by cherub musicians playing strange harps. The left panel was a medieval Christ gesturing with two fingers and staring nonlocally with black eyes. The right panel was the bat-signal-over-Metropolis dove of the Holy Spirit.

You covered the three panels of the triptych with tin foil and set me in front of the trio of mirrors like a debutante freshly introduced to her Victorian toilet stand. You moved the two side panels to ninety-degree positions. You told me to look. You said

look for your true image

where are you?

and I
looked and I looked as you eased the Holy Spirit mirror
out to 91°, 92°, 93°, and I saw my face bending its infinite
replicas into a vista of crinkled aluminum and realized
   would never know where   was aga n...

   am gone from your s ght, am gone from your v s on, am
gone from your hope, am gone from th s page, such gl tter-
ng fragments of the worldly the world the word made crash.

48.

Of course, you had many lessons to teach me with images,
sweet sister. You introduced me to porno. Remember this?
You stole skin mags for me from the drugstore when you
went to steal nail polish for yourself. We took them to the
choir loft and hid in the pipe chamber. You opened the
pages with the grace of a midwife holding an anatomical
primer. There were women impossibly shaped. There were
women splayed across the hoods of expensive cars. There
were women performing strange contortions in front of
mirrors. There were women washing their buttocks with
huge gobs of lather while standing in low wooden barrels
in the desert. There were women in purple rooms holding
plastic cocks like altar boys carrying candlesticks. The
camera did not seem to be interested in the ear or the
neck. There were women awaiting gynaecological examinations from invisible incubi. These women sometimes
looked fearful. How enticing. Rachel Gabriel Rosie. Bambi
Annie Liz. (— In a caption, Stella says "I LOVE seamen
— I see men, and I eat 'em.") There were women wearing
rubber stockings. (— "I'm lonely.") There were women in
replicas of ancient costume, made out to be queens, ladies
in waiting, slave-girls with perms, jungle nymphs with
skin-coloured nylons and manicures. Caveman porn:
women in acrylic leopard skin holding styrofoam clubs.
There were women bent over and staring out of the page
from between their tense thighs and hanging breasts, their

alabaster bums forming triumphal arches for the twin columns of their inverted stare. There were sawed off cocks sticking in from the edge of the frames suggesting an artillery of telescopic gazes. Some of these cocks were bent upwards like bows. Some of these cocks seemed to be bruised. There were women who were shaved in obvious places to give them the appearance of little girls. (— "Petite Cindy forgot her panties in the change room. O no, Cindy, whatever will you do? — **spread-em, bitch-girl! Beg me to pull your pigtails hard!**") There were women preyed on by three men at the same time. (— "I'm just not satisfied until **three big cocks** are filling *all* my wet holes!") There were women receiving geysers of semen into their mouths with feigned ecstasy. There were women whose flesh had the texture of poorly bled pork. Their blemishes had been airbrushed. (— "I'm lonely.") There were women in congress with domestic animals. Women in Star-Trek costumes getting it from behind by Klingons or space monsters with polyurethane masks. Caption under space-porn spread: "**Meet Divula X, sucker of inter-planetary missiles!**" There were women dressed in tuxedoes and holding bullwhips. (— "Wanna scream, big guy?") There were women pinching each other's labia with such sharp fingernails that I crossed my legs and squeezed.

getting hard little brother?
And then you brought out from the fold of your smock a pyx of holy chrism. You uncapped it and poured a bead into my open hand.

go on jerk off. but start slowly.
Obedient by nature. I unzipped and withdrew my small penis and began to rub. Liza Kathy Michelle. And then the International Pages. Kay-Lee from China (San Francisco) with pretty bound feet. Mumbulla from Kenya (Harlem) with a plastic bone in her nose. Gayatri from India (Baltimore) lifting her orange and yellow sari. Fatima from Iran (Cleveland) with wedding belt of gold coins and a red silk veil. I saw an ad for a penis enlarger. I saw an ad for a penis whip: "leave a lasting impression". I

saw women quarantined to the post-advertisement pages, guilty of possessing stretch marks. (— "I'm **so** lonely. I need some **attention**.") They looked sad. (— "Cherrie is divorced with two kids but she still loves to fuck. Are you still **breast-feeding**, Cherrie? LUCKY KIDS! WOULD-N'T YOU LIKE TO SUCK ON THOSE TITS, BOYS?")

— I'm lonely. —

look at their eyes don't they all look like me? brown eyes pale blue look at this mirror (you open your compact and show me my twisted face), *see how your eyes are filled with the same empty space* (you strike a match and hold it between my face and the mirror), *and do you see now how your pupils contract with the flame? that's the rub. kid in the lights of cameras your mind filters out what's important. you lose their backdrops you see only their silhouettes. silhouettes are unholy. shapes are unholy. anything two-dimensional is unholy. this is why i have brought you to this place of shadow and depth true love is tenebral* (I had no idea what you were talking about. Best to keep wanking.) *if you ever come across these pages in bright light and you feel desire you will have sinned does my wisdom fill your mouth with countless angelic nipples?*

YES! YES! OH YES VERONICA! I cried, on the verge of spunking. Then you slapped the magazine shut and stood up and leapt away from my breathing and threw back the veil on a wood panel leaning up against a bank of slanting organ pipes. It was an icon... danse macabre... one wreathed skeleton pulling a young monk towards a grave over which a second skeleton stands holding a spade and grinning... cut into walnut by a Dutch Jansenist in 1482... My erection collapsed, detonating from a fuse of anti-rapture lodged deep like a rusty spring-locked IUD.

what's the matter. little one?

grushabbbabalshisst...

what's wrong? o hell. don't cry. idiot child i

have only shown you the disparities i have only shown you ugliness to teach you beauty. i have only shown you the unexplainable incisions. the chasms. those cliffs upon which the sun comes up like anne frank and goes down like the whore of babylon i've only played leonard cohen 8-tracks so you could hear the osmonds more clearly. stop snivelling i'm talking to you i have not given you anything but an armour of scars i give you these pictures as holy cards you must erase their evil and start again all right?

shnorflekububbleplufffsh o God ,Veronica, your face.

what about my face?

I-I can't look at those pictures ever again. Your face is everywhere.

~~good~~ you said and then we took the magazines down out of the loft and slipped them through the sewer grate on Bond Street. A wino looked up and then went back to eating grass.

Record rains fell that spring and the sewage overflowed. The pages were pushed up and out onto the pavement by swells of fetid water so that when next we saw those pictures they were plastered in every disposition all over the concrete. Some had floated up through the cathedral gates into the courtyard like two-dimensional Magdalens clamouring for forgiveness. The ink ran down from their painted faces to cover with improvised modesty their beautiful breasts. The sun came out. Small boys very much like myself stood mutely over the images, looking, looking.

49.

Pottery

The word that came to Jeremiah from the Lord: 'Arise, and go down to the potter's house, and there I will let you hear my words.' So I went down to the potter's house, and there he was working at his wheel. And the vessel he was making of clay was spoiled in the potter's hands, and he reworked it into another vessel. (Jeremiah 18: 1-4)

Our mother works with clay. She rounds it, places it in the centre of the wheel, and steps down on the treadle. Moistens her hands from a bowl on the counter. Clouded water drips to her apron like milk. Her palms hiss against the form like a fine rain. The sound makes me close my eyes. The world is pouring water from one hand to the other. Veronica, you are reading a book in the corner. My hands smell of lead. Our father stumbles around upstairs with his eyes in his hand. Our mother catches herself humming the same tune four hours after hearing it on the radio. There are shards of red clay on the floor. Plaster dust covers the windows.

I open my eyes. I gaze upon the spinning vessel, her thumbs plunging into the neck, hollowing. There is a spiral motif that my eyes follow downwards into the wheel. My body warms with the spinning room, conducting friction from the bowels of a divided earth, one side spinning against another in the breached birth of Time, Gravity and Masochism, the motion carving grooves to guide runoff water, and to be read by the blind of another age.

Veronica turns a page in her book.

50.

Once, mother let me choose a glass bead for the eye of a peacock in the rose window. I chose a bead that was perfectly clear. I've since plucked it out with my pocketknife, having decided that the clearest clear is the prettiest nothing. — The hole whistles A' with an E" overtone when the wind blows from the north. In the winter the bottom lip of the hole grows a long tear of ice. When the ice-tear melts, the water runs down over the tail of a bird-of-paradise, then over a bunch of grapes, a pear, an apple, and plaited vines, to rest against the lip of the wooden frame, where it teases the wood towards its destiny of rotting. — When the window collapses, as all windows must, it'll be because of the empty peacock eye.

51.

Although they gave us names and let us eavesdrop on their quiet and sad occupations and so forth, "mom" and "dad" are as accidental as stories from books chosen randomly from a ruined library.

They died absurdly. Our mother had just completed the last section of the rose window. Our Father was helping her install it. They stood on thin planks of scaffolding. A sparrow fluttered in through the frame. Our Father was thrown off balance. He grasped at her and pulled her with him. I imagine Our Mother smiled in her flight. (— To my knowlege, our legal codes make no provision to classify the murderer of someone who may not have minded. —) I found them heaped brokenly in a pool of blood when I came in to practice the organ. The blood obscured the mosaic. I ran back to tell you, Veronica. You were not surprised. I phoned the ambulance. You began to pack a duffel bag. You said *see you around* Then you walked out past the marquee of ambulances and squad cars into the spring.

I turned my attention to music. I was destined to become the cathedral organist. I had learned the entire repertoire of Bach when next I heard from you. It was a thin replacement. Beauty heals nothing.

52.

Once I was at mass. During the homily I walked out for a smoke by the church gate. This beefy dark-haired guy comes out and lights up a butt beside me. He's the one who hands out bulletins before mass (sponsored by the advertising of various funeral homes) and helps old ladies to their seats and holds the poorbox in the lobby at the end. We inhale. — A sparrow lands on the courtyard grotto and tilts its head. — We exhale.

I say, Nice day isn't it.

Fuckin great.

Beats February.

Yep.

Yep.

Yessir.

Yipperoo.

Uhn-huh.

[Pause.]

Father Sean is a good man, I offer.

Huh?

Father Sean is a good man. A good speaker.

I haven't listened to a homily in years. Too many words.

Oh.

So let's make the most of not listening and cut the motherfuckin rag chewin.

What?

You heard me, you faggot. I'se in no mood for fuckin the dog.

[Long pause]

I was amazed. I continued tentatively, seaching for the Safe Topic:

So, um, uh, what's your summer going to be like? I asked.

Well I gotta full agenda but I dunno what I'm doin. Guess I'll keep on workin with my group.

What group is that?

"Schizophrenics R Us" (flashing a MedicAlert bracelet).

I nod, simulating universal comprehension. He drops his butt, steps on it, closes his voided eyes.

I don't have to work, y'know. I got CPP and disability benefits from my accident. Didja hear about my accident? I'm famous for it. Man, it was some **ACCIDENT**. It was **THE ACCIDENT**. I'm only tellin you this cause I think ya know about accidents, buddy. Or y'should know. I assure ya you've had an accident. I kin tell. Ya look like a man who wanted to be a hero and then ya missed the audition. Ya got that I've-been-wounded-and-I-don't-know-why-because-I-know-fuckall-about-God look. Ya see the way it is Jack is like this. Ya can settle down, have a wife an kids an a house an a car an another goddamn car for sunday an eat beans an shit regular an watch hockey an buy a cemetery plot an whatall. It's either one thing or another thing an that other thing is allus gonna be better than the first thing, whichya don' even know about cause that first thing hasn't happened yet. What I'm sayin is is that the only bumfuck constant in this here world Jack is **ACCIDENTS.** That firs thing is a accident. Jesus wept and HE CAN'T STOP. Man, He knew bout accidents. What a fuckin **ACCIDENT.** Who knows what my spirit came from but whatever I came from I know where I'm going, an you an I will wind up by accidental intention inna same place an that place is the accidental home of **absolute nothing**, which isn't only a place but also's what I do with my God-given time an do you know what I jus found out? Do you know what I know? I figgered it out yesterday. Here it is Jack, all the glory you can handle: **ABSOLUTE NOTHING IS SOMETHING TO BEHOLD.**

53.

An accidental is a chromatically altered note in a musical composition that is usually foreign to the key indicated by the signature. An accidental will appear in a musical text to introduce either a key modulation or a change of modality from, for example, major to minor. The effect of this indication is limited to the measure of music in which it is inscribed. The bar line cancels the effect of the accidental. Thus, musical texts make internal provision for the erasure of their accidents. Outside of music, accidents are contained by no such safeguard. — Our parents lived and died without music. Their deaths were listed as *accidental* in the coroner's book.

)　　*

---

* This sign has thus far been used as a performative narrative/thematic breathmark. In this instance, however, it indicates the passage of real silent time. The narrator has just been separated from his object of desire, i.e., his sister, addressee, communicant, surrogate reader. He is taken in by the cathedral rectory and eats his meals with retired priests who ask him to pass the butter in latin. I don't remember much about that time. My room had a large 1890's window in it with rippling panes of Victorian glass but I kept the curtains drawn in self-consciousness. — He also kept his door locked because he felt the gaze of Fr. Oldgrave to be of questionable intent. — In viewing this comma we should think of the "lost years" of every literary character's life. In biblical and hagiographical treatments, these lacunae are usually glossed over with the sentence "so-and-so lived and grew in grace and was filled with the Holy Spirit." Things aren't so simple here. I don't remember much about that time. The narrator doesn't remember much about that time. Somebody told me they saw Veronica streetwalking down on Jarvis: "Your sister makes a goodlookin whore. She sucked my cock for five bucks. Usually I pay ten." — Evidently I remember a few things. Most things were vague. The sky was never quite blue nor quite grey nor quite any of the grades of fire we see in the sunset. I definitely remember waiting by the mailbox in the grey mornings, for a letter, from, I don't know, somebody.

54.

dear little one,

i have been out of touch for too long. sorry, i've been in too many places to even begin to describe so i'm just writing to let you know that i've decided to become a nun. i take my vows tomorrow. the abbess will marry me to christ with a tiny golden ring, like this:

love,
veronica, novice, d.m.

p.s. are you still studying music? how's the rectory? give fr. oldgrave my best regards.

55.

You became a nun, Sister. It was simple, and to be expected. We have both known people to do the unexplainable — to hear particular songs and then leap like swans from bridges to be impaled by shimmering stalactites of ice. Perfectly happy people walking into Toronto harbour with their pockets filled with sand. We understand the random glory.

That you are suddenly a nun in isolation is not a matter of narrative convenience. It's a fact. As much a fact as me being who I say I am.

(— Doves fly between television antennae and disrupt nature programming...)

56.

You converted many. You exhorted your sisters to higher aims. You had visions of stigmata. You were quiet about this and then people found out. As always, the scant coverage afforded by the media only increased the pathos:

57.*

Veronica, you once said *i am a fish, a beautiful fish, a dolphin, yes a dolphin* — Allow me to dream your present ocean, your convent. Hopefully, I will manage to recover the few patterns of catholic devotional practice I find to be honourable. (— So many things are passing away. There goes that bird into the open subway vent. There goes the sun behind that incinerator.) — Mark the sadness of the fabular form.

---

*"We are now prepared to consider the more direct part which worms take in the denudation of the land...". Charles Darwin, *The Formation of Vegetable Mould through the Action of Worms with Observations on their Habits*, London, 1881.

58.

Once there was a convent, gardens of bending, crops of time, ploughshare and scythe glinting idle at the hour of prayer. Leathered hands clasp, gnarl and wither. Orchards where arms stretched up and ladders were steadied from underneath. Roof of thatch, roof of stone, roof of slate and copper, lit by the moon in one age, by passing headlights in another. Many nuns walked through fields in the waning light. Many nuns lay awake listening to rain on the strange roof. Their cloaks hung in closets, they kissed each other tenderly. In the third week of every month they washed their stained cloths in the same basin, and emptied the rosed water at the edge of a corn field.

Catastrophes were unreadable signs.

There were floods in the spring. The water fouled with the corpses of drowned sheep. The Mother Superior calmly steered a raft between pillars of the basilica, the baptismal font beneath her like a stone anchor. She floated through the clerestory windows, out over the fields, looking down to see the wheat wave gently below. The tabernacle surfaced, turned over in the sun, slowly filled with water as its air and chalices displaced, then sank again. Pigments from the scriptorium billowed up like internal bleeding. The bodies of drowned nuns floated on the surface for many days, their skins chafing against cut glass mosaics high on submerged walls. Some months later, the waters receded, and dysentery struck many of the surviving nuns. They squatted in the mud and wept.

There were fires in late summer. Sows bolted through plank doors, milk boiling in seared udders. Women ran into the forest with flaming hair. The elderly burning peacefully in their beds. The marble of the chapel altar polished itself in the heat.

Once a fire destroyed all the books. The generation of initiates at that time became painters and dancers and actors. The unburnt shelves of the library were taken down and the boards were used to build stages with platforms and trap doors. The books that arrived in replacement were written in a different language. Within a single lifetime the old language disappeared, though the painters and dancers heard it spoken in dreams. One nun watched two thousand typed pages of her little devotional poems, written over sixty years, feed the flames. Walking through the ashes with bare feet, she decided to become a musician, and looked through the smouldering beams for a soundboard.

Periods of relative peace were spent documenting periods of chaos.*

There was a monastery near by, and by night the swallows would fly between the two roofs of clay tile. On many occasions a monk and a nun would gaze at each other across fields of sunflowers. One would leave a rosary in the knot of a tree for the other to pray by. One winter morning one such pair were found curled around each other on the bank of the pond that separated the properties. They were frozen to death, a heel of bread in her hand, his cloak pulled over their faces.

One nun painted icons of the Virgin holding the Child. One day, many years after her menstruation had stopped, milk began to flow from her breasts. She went to the Mother, holding her arms over the stains on her cloak. Mother prescribed a balm of herbs. When this failed, the nun was sent to the orphanage to work as a wet-nurse. She died while feeding. Another sister came into the room and removed the suckling infant from her cooling body.

There were many visions imagined. A nun dreams about Mary Magdalen bleeding from the mouth as she says Master. A nun walks through the woods and sees a wolf devouring a swallow and the wolf changes into St. Paul

---

* "Archaeologists are probably not aware how much they owe to worms from the preservation of many ancient objects. Coins, gold ornaments, stone implements, etc., if dropped on the surface of the ground, will infallibly be buried by the castings of worms in a few years, and will thus be safely preserved, until the land at some future time is turned up..."
— Darwin, ibid.

before her eyes. An oak tree bears plums. A swordfish is found flopping on the bank of the freshwater pond. A sister sings a song in Aramaic and everyone understands. A novice comes to confession, claiming guilt for having consented with a rose bush. For ten years the phone in the chapel sacristy rings on Holy Saturday at six in the evening. When it is answered there is silence.

(Many mysteries remain hidden from general knowledge. If the world was told of every mystery with which it was complicit, it would go mad, for the language surrounding the world would suddenly come from inside itself, and the bridge between speaking and hearing would be swept away by a glowing ozone river. The consequences would be similar if you yourself spontaneously recite the most beautiful poem you had yet heard.)

There were fewer real visions involving supernatural contact. Jesus came to one nun in the form of her mother, and braided her hair in the dawn. The sisters examined the braid, unable to tell whether it contained three or four strands. The braid remained bound through her years, all her new hair growing into it. When she died it was cut from her scalp and laid in a glass box. Another report describes how the entire cloister witnessed the colour of the altar flowers seep through their stems and pool at the base of the marble pillars. In memory of this miracle every nun is given a white ceramic rose on the jubilee of her vow.

Less often than the imagined visions, yet more often than the real ones, sisters were raped. One rapist carried a quiver of arrows and drank from a goatskin; another wore an ammunition belt and drank from an aluminum can. Sometimes there were two or three other men with him, and the sister would be held open on the ground, her back against gnarled roots.

The raped sister would stumble into the convent, in shock, speechless, her tongue bleeding. If she was too shamed to tell her sisters the story, and if she could hide her wounds, she slipped into her cell and sent word to the

Mother that she was ill and could not attend Vespers. She would wash the blood from her cope with water from the eavestrough outside her window. Over the following weeks she would brew teas of bitter herbs in the hope of poisoning her womb. — If the nun could not hide her bleeding and regained enough language to tell of the attack, she was taken to the infirmary. Her habit was washed with the other habits. (— Only the faintest stain was noticeable as it billowed on the line with the others.) She was monitored carefully. If her menstruation stopped and she became sick in the mornings, she was placed in solitude until her time came. The baby was given to a local family, and the knowledge was absorbed into the woodgrain of prie-dieux. Not uncommonly, that baby was a girl and that girl would arrive at the threshold of the convent fifteen years later, asking to take vows. In these cases her mother recognized her flesh, and either hid from the girl, or constructed excuses to spend unusual amounts of time with her. Sometimes the story was unveiled by the touch of a hand on a cheek.

One night the Mother Superior lay awake in her cell after prayer and said aloud: *The world is a sin, the sinner is sorry, we are here to channel apologies to the ear beyond the world.*

They were as the offspring of swallows that nest in bell-towers, hatched deaf from the iron music, but singing nonetheless. — When the Bishop came, they knelt in rows on either side of the front path, from the chapel to where his carriage or limousine stopped. He held out his right hand as he passed. They reached for it tenderly, and kissed his ring.

They were teachers and poets and singers and painters. They ran shelters for battered women. Public officials approved of this charity that they themselves were unwilling to offer. The nuns offered blankets and soup to trembling victims, saying *You catch your peace now and if you want to tell us about your trouble, do so when you feel safe.*

Here, let me wash your face, the doctor will be here soon. They were midwives for rape victims. They sewed cords of canvas to bind the limbs of heroin addicts to iron-railed detox beds. They travelled to war zones, translating prayers into the diplomacy of foreign tongues. When they made too much peace they were shot. The world is combustible, discharging into the breasts of those who possess inordinate light. — Mother Superior received unsigned notices from the offices of dictatorships.

Their serene faces in the street caused many to sublimate a belief in a safe world: that sanctuary was everywhere, that the universe was responsive.

In the late twentieth century, the world began to roll away with itself like a man who speaks only because he is confused as to whether he is alive or dead. Social theorists began to *enjoy* speaking of entropy and decay. Demons became more obvious in their manipulation of technology. Before long the nuns were not, and when they were they were not as they were before. And although nothing ever is, nothing became their way.

Fewer ventured out into the cities to do their work, because fewer could overcome their fear of a world folding into itself to examine its own entrails, while having lost both the power of augury and the ability to weep. A single generation of nuns aged together, with no inheritors. Because fewer could work, less of their land could be maintained. They brought less corn to the market. They had no surplus of wheat. Their staple became the communion bread they had once sent out for the masses of the diocese. They sold an empty cloister building to the public school system. Within a year, the principal had metal detectors installed at the entrances because fifteen-year-olds were bringing handguns to school. One day a senile nun entered the building by mistake, looking for her cell. The wire chain of her rosary set off alarms. A police officer guided her home, holding her arm gently.

The nuns began to use the chapel. They sold the church to an industrialist. He poured concrete into the crypt to stabilize the foundation. He stood on a pile of gravel where the Altar of Repose had been and spat into the dust, dreaming of happy production. He ripped out the marble tiles and the altars and everything that would obstruct his machines. Before long scavengers found lecterns and lavabos and misereres in the city dump, where the gulls circled in cold compass-arcs.*

The nuns used the money from the sold property to convert the remaining buildings into a nursing home. They installed handrails in the hallways. They bought walkers and wheelchairs. They hired a doctor and several nurses, and converted the smaller chapel into an examination room. They turned the wine cellar into a refrigerator room and began to stock it with bags of blood gathered at clinics held on the second Wednesday of every month. Cousins and nephews came to visit their religious relatives and to give blood.

They installed a camera in the choir loft of the chapel to beam the office and mass to every cell of the chronic care ward. The image of the altar hovered on channel eight 24 hours a day. At night only the sanctuary lamp was visible, its flame burning the pixels of one hundred screens left on through the night while the heart monitors beeped. Channel 7 played news. Channel 9 played videos.

Time did not heed them. They spent their lives dismantling clocks built in Babylon, and time did not heed them. They made the hands and the gears into icons by which the emptiness of time could be envisioned, and time did not heed them. They fell out of time and into graves dug

---

* "We may conclude from these facts that when the abbey was destroyed and the stones removed, a layer of rubbish was left over the whole surface, and that as soon as the worms were able to penetrate the decayed concrete and the joints between the tiles, they slowly filled up the interstices in the overlying rubbish with their castings, which were afterwards accumulated to a thickness of nearly three inches over the whole surface…" — Darwin, ibid.

between strands of fibre optics, and time did not heed them. The history of the world recorded time in a mathematics of antipathy, inscribing the hours and names in black ledgers that looked like the black habits of deceased nuns folded away in oak cabinets.

In the year of Our Lord nineteen hundred and eighty nine a comely young woman of unknown history and a quiet but wise disposition came to the convent, giving her name to be Veronica and expressing her desire to forsake world and flesh for devotion to God, who, she explained, she suspected to be dangling in just such a place like a bellringer in a ruined tower, hanging on for nothing but to hear the last echoes of a beautiful original ring. She handed her small shoulder bag to the matron. She was allowed to retain her comb and toothbrush. She was given the garb of a novice and a psalter bound in red leather. She was assigned menial jobs.

Before long this Veronica befriended an invalid sister, with whom she would sit in the grey afternoons. They prayed together through the televised mass, listening to the singing of two hundred elderly women. They prayed the rosary together. Veronica sang the old hymns in a young voice, for which she was appreciated.

One day, she took the old nun out for a walk around the grounds the convent had managed to retain. A colostomy bag hung from the arm of the old woman's wheelchair.* It was fed by a tube emerging from under her blanket. While they walked through the descending winter, it collected pink urine and yellow feces. They stopped by a wood, and

---

* "The floors of the old rooms, halls and passages have generally sunk, partly from the settling of the ground, but chiefly from having been undermined by worms; and the sinking has commonly been greater in the middle than near the walls. The walls themselves, whenever their foundations do not lie at a great depth, have been penetrated and undermined by worms, and have consequently subsided. The unequal subsidence thus caused probably explains the great cracks which may be seen in many ancient walls, as well as their inclination away from the perpendicular..."
— Darwin, ibid.

the old woman told Veronica the Latin names of all the trees, some of which she had planted over seventy years before. She had been trained as a biologist.

When they returned to the infirmary, Veronica closed the door behind them like a hatch against the air. *The old woman said The world is changing. I used to be able to understand the change by examining fossils. But now the fossils are all uncovered and their prophecies hold no interest. Perhaps I am a fossil. Are you interested in fossils, Veronica?*

yes i am.

Then the old nun told Veronica a story about the Flood, speaking the logic of erosion: *You know, Sister Veronica, all the condemned creatures did not die at the same time. Because God used water instead of fire, those that lived in the waters survived for generations, simply rearranging the boundaries of home. Crystalline trout streams and salmon runs were lost in deep sea waters. Freshwater fish learned to mate in coral reefs. Many natural enemies disappeared. The corpses of gulls and hawks sank through towering watery forests towards their submerged nests, some of which still held their eggs, bloating and cracking with the rot of drowned embryos. The fish lived long enough to watch the corpses settle. Their offspring knew nothing except the death of the world, thinking that they alone had been saved or that things had always been like this, and they would swim forever in the blue museum, which was theirs to study and discuss. But over many years they too were enfeebled, their oxygen eaten by the putrefaction of dead bodies and vegetation returning to lifeless slime. Rising poisons from the bowels of the earth. Rank bubbles drifting up past the gills, opening at the surface to feed a stinking sky. The fish were allowed their lives only to watch life die.*

Veronica, this is the way I feel sometimes, that I have spent my life examining things whose death will kill me as well. I have watched Catholic angels fall through water like those hawks towards their nests. Sometimes I look up, and see the shadow of an ark passing over me. Veronica, there is always a flood. God will never use fire. And there will always be those left behind to tell the stories that will kill them.

59.

The long bow of my body, left by a mute hunter who has retreated into caves to nurse a lonely hunger.

I lean against the stone-cold drywall and look out through the kitchen window. The cup of my shoulder turns to metal and siphons the ice. The fires of winter smoulder in trash cans. All the lawyers are hard at work. Today is a bad day for TV.

Yesterday, however, I saw this nature show. It was about songbirds. I thought it was totally appropriate that the ornithologists just can't figure out why songbirds migrate.

They return to northern Ontario in April, having flown 9,000 kilometres from various equitorial oases. They stop in central Mexico, Texas, and Kansas. Some veer east, lighting upon our fair city's High Park in fatigue and near starvation. Fifty million birds pass through each of the main arborial pitstops per day, over a two-week period. Two hundred and fifty species are represented in the migration. And now, in 1994, only half the numbers are flying as when the ornithologists started counting and tagging them in '63. No one knows why the numbers are diminishing.

The average male songbird sings over ten thousand times a day.

The show featured clips of a volunteer bird counter and his wife who have been assigned a 40-kilometre stretch of northbound highway to monitor each spring on behalf of the Canadian Songbird Preservation Society. They climb out of the van at intervals of 800 metres, she with a clipboard and stopwatch, he with binoculars. He is given three minutes to name all of the birds within earshot. "Begin", she says, clicking the stopwatch. He calls out.
TWO RED-BREASTED WOODTHRUSH

FOUR, NO, FIVE MORNING DOVES OVERHEAD
ONE CATBIRD

THREE LYREBIRD

ONE PARADISE HAUNTER

THREE GREENBACK FINCHES I THINK, NO, IT'S FIVE, I'M SURE IT'S FIVE and "Stop", she says, jotting the last entry. He never uses the binoculars, but cups his hands to his ears. Interviewed later, he says *Well, each bird has its own song, and they're all quite different. Some even use different dialects for different reasons. Anyone can learn these languages if they really desire.*

60.

Veronica, this dream has music. Very fragile, very human. Have you been hearing it?

Veronica, I became the cathedral organist! After so many years! I practice at night and remember you during the day. I mount the spiral steps and smell the lingering musk of our trysts. — I see a streetlamp through the empty peacock eye. — I throw the ancient switch. I listen for the great intake of air like those made by the cooling fans of particle accelerators. I conduct a choir of little boys. They line up like blowup sex dolls perpetually mouthing full-lipped O's. — I command a full complement of 3,694 pipes. I have been the aural overseer of 2,012 weddings and 2,198 funerals. I am more necessary than incense. If it weren't for me, the mass would be a shitty poetry reading conducted by men in stupid hats. My improvisations are legendary. Everyone is astonished that I have but two hands. I decided to spend my life making music within the Church. You, however, being easily bored, left our home to sing outside, with your whole body, not restricted as I was to the fingertips. I learned to play the organ while you learned to fuck. I learned to balance on the bench while you learned to arch your back and squeeze your vaginal walls with exquisite precision, reciting the Kama Sutra of St. Maria Maddalena de' Pazzi, c. 1580, a Carmelite nun with a classic tendency to self-torture... rolling in thorn bushes... wearing prickly undies... lashing herself with nettles and whips... consuming nothing but Holy Communion, extra Blood for dessert... seizing statues of Jesus, stripping all the drapes and trappings, hollering for him to be naked... the word "love" caused her paroxysms of excitement: 𝕺 𝕷𝖔𝖗𝖉, 𝖒𝖞 𝕲𝖔𝖉, 𝖎𝖙 𝖎𝖘 𝖊𝖓𝖔𝖚𝖌𝖍, 𝖎𝖙 𝖎𝖘 𝖊𝖓𝖔𝖚𝖌𝖍, 𝖎𝖙 𝖎𝖘 𝖙𝖔𝖔 𝖒𝖚𝖈𝖍, 𝕺 𝕵𝖊𝖘𝖚𝖘... 𝕺 𝕲𝖔𝖉 𝖔𝖋 𝕷𝖔𝖛𝖊, 𝖓𝖔, 𝕴 𝖈𝖆𝖓 𝖓𝖊𝖛𝖊𝖗 𝖘𝖙𝖔𝖕 𝖋𝖗𝖔𝖒 𝖈𝖗𝖞𝖎𝖓𝖌 𝖔𝖋 𝖑𝖔𝖛𝖊... 𝕺 𝖑𝖔𝖛𝖊, 𝖞𝖔𝖚 𝖆𝖗𝖊 𝖒𝖊𝖑𝖙𝖎𝖓𝖌 𝖆𝖓𝖉 𝖉𝖎𝖘-𝖘𝖔𝖑𝖛𝖎𝖓𝖌 𝖒𝖞 𝖛𝖊𝖗𝖞 𝖇𝖊𝖎𝖓𝖌. 𝖄𝖔𝖚 𝖆𝖗𝖊 𝖈𝖔𝖓𝖘𝖚𝖒𝖎𝖓𝖌 𝖆𝖓𝖉 𝖐𝖎𝖑𝖑𝖎𝖓𝖌 𝖒𝖊.... 𝕺𝖍 𝖈𝖔𝖒𝖊, 𝖈𝖔𝖒𝖊, 𝖆𝖓𝖉 𝖑𝖔𝖛𝖊, 𝖑𝖔𝖛𝖊... (— All the while I sat in the loft, dreaming of Quasimodo and rolling out arpeggios at the keyboard... ladders of unscalable harmony...) Your cult... meetings on Friday nights... novenas... relics of vaginal secretions... paten pasties... candlestick dildoes... a black market of flagra, hairshirts, prickly girdles and anatomically explicit icons... The Holy Riol Grrl Cartel. O Ronnie, did you get your wish? Are you the Abbess of the Holy Sisters of Sexual Mortification? Is your Motherhouse on Sunset Strip? Does its sign flicker with chasers and neon palm trees that blink into gartered legs? Are you being scourged right now by the youngest and prettiest novice who shakes her head sobbing no mother nonono? Are you crying out with pleasure right now, as I, your frustrated bachelor, string the rope on my chasuble unnecessarily tight and try to remember which descant to play for the opening hymn of the mass on this fine and sunny morning of the Feast of the Immaculate Conception?

61.

Once there was a Choirboy who sang so fervently that he went deaf. Because of his deafness his voice split: those around him could hear one of his voices, and only he could hear the other. The two voices sang duets for angels to assemble and God to decipher. His outer voice was a parallel life, intimately connected to his, but unknowable. (Although sometimes we see what we cannot know, as when leaves appear to rustle on only one branch of a tree.)

His deafness is a metaphor for his sister's thunder.

The chinese ideogram for singing depicts a human mouth hovering beside a bird. Such gentle ventriloquism between species.

Once my sister and I played a clapping game. We sat on a mattress in an alley while a man with a bleeding forehead slept whimpering in a pool of urine. We sang the same rhyme, co-oblivious with the world, playing among bottleshard angels in our cinderblock heaven. My sister and I looked so much alike. I imagined I was singing to a mirror. Before long I couldn't tell whose voice was whose. But by that time the object of the game had changed to seeing which of us could make the other's hands sting. — The man's forehead was like bark oozing sap. He moaned Martha I fuckin hate you you fuckin bitch.

A story in the apocrypha of the Old Testament has it that Jonah learned how to sing by listening to his own echo in the belly of the whale. He wedged himself in the esophagus to avoid the stomach acids. He hummed a little. A few doo-de-doo-de-doooos. Tralala. Mimimeeeee. His voice returned in echo, resonating in the labyrinth of intestinal walls, Romanesque cages of rib and cartilage. Slowly, he worked up to words, his voice amplified by confidence and solitude. He remembered verses, the rhyming koans of ascetics, temple responsories, law charters, the tally of his sanhedrin tithings, sacrifice schedules, dreidl songs... He sang the words slowly, the cold flesh pressing his back and arms like a dead mother. When he was spat out onto the beach, his tunic eaten through with whale-bile, he found himself blind. He became a cantor in the temple and the people regarded him as an upright man. He never spoke aloud of the ordeal.

Once I dreamt of the sound of resurrection. I sat for hours in an airless tomb, and then the bloody body of my slain Lord began to glow, foetally. The dream was full of cheesy sci-fi effects, but this made it even more believable. Fluorescence climbing the walls, the wash of a single synthesized note pouring through the limestone. I dreamt there was a sealed room behind the far wall that was banked with the chaser lights of useless dashboards, and scrolls of paper black with binary code rolling out of humming printers. The Star of Harmonics expanded in my chest. (The word sublime comes to the lungs in its tired way. The dream dreams of a new windpipe through which to sound it.)

In 1937, Louis Vierne, a French organist who was blind from birth, gave a recital of original compositions at Cathédral Sacre-Coeur in Paris. Poor old Louis suffered a fatal heart attack while playing the final piece — an improvisation on a Gregorian psalmody — and slumped against the manuals of the instrument, the stops of which were still drawn. Five minutes passed before the audience realized that the sustained chord produced by the corpse was not a foreseen part of the performance. How many years will it take for our audience to understand this about us?

62.

THE ORGAN BENCH, or BALANCING WITH VARIOUS AVATARS OF CHRIST ON THE THANATIC TIGHTROPE STRUNG OVER THE BLACK HOLE BETWEEN TWIN VANTAGE POINTS OF SILENCE AND HOWLING.

In the February 1980 issue of *Hustler* magazine there appears a cartoon in which a man is being operated upon. A huge-breasted nurse (her perfectly round cartoon-nipples half-peeping out of her low-cut uniform), is holding a miniature pipe organ over the patient's gaping abdomen. The caption says "Organ Transplant." I was nine in February of 1980. It was the same year I began to study the organ. I also gave my first confession that year.

My organ teacher informed me that balance was the organist's greatest asset. He commanded me to balance on the bench. *It's like swimming*, he said, *your legs and arms moving against the currents of pedal and keyboard. Keep your back straight or you'll drown.*

Committed to art, my teacher committed suicide. He fell through the carillon tower with impeccable balance. His fall made the bells ring. The hobos heard this. It was their custom to read time and begging schedules from the bells. They wandered to the church gates to panhandle from mass-goers, but there was nobody there. They returned to their parking lots. They kneeled at the sides of cars, unscrewing the gascaps to inhale the fumes. Their image suggested prayerfulness to me one day and fellatio the next.

I became a pole-sitter for music. It was my refuge from you, sister. Mother gazed up at my lamplight through her rose window. She begged me to descend. She stood in her night-gown in the courtyard and called my name through the window at three in the morning. I called back to her. The window did not change colour with the passage of our voices.

As in the story of St. Benedict in the desert, a cat brought me bread and a dove brought me water in those lonely hours. A crow sent me off to sleep by upsetting the hourglass on the music stand with the sweep of a black wing. The glass shattered and the white sand spilled. By the glinting light of these shards I read the tracks of the crow's feet in the sand. These were the last notes I read before succumbing to the noteless with my forehead against the keyboards. I regularly dreamt that my body was hollow.

I began by studying the music of Dietrich Buxtehude, the teacher of Bach. I read that he took only three organ students at a time. He chose beggar children from the alleyways of Stuttgart by looking at their palms. He would say 𝕳ello little boy, if you hold out your hand 𝕴 will give you a piece of sugared pig's ear. The ragged child would hold out his palm. Dietrich looked at it carefully, to see whether the line that predicted parenthood suggested infertility, but held the promise of a sixth finger, the one that would add that missing voice to the incomplete music of the world. Once accepted as students, their monthly examinations consisted partly of this same palmistry. Their hands would be examined for new lines. Dietrich was con-vinced that the undisciplined hand could reveal the mistakes that would plague the student for the rest of his life. When the boys entered the age of desire, Dietrich taught them how to masturbate with open fingers to avoid cramping. He was convinced that playing an instrument with a gentle hand was akin to touching oneself without the clenching of desperation. The music, he asserted, must not be chafed or bruised while its seed sprays forth in glittering arcs. — Dietrich was famous for his disciplinary methods. He forced his students to have wooden crosses bound to their spines, their arms outstretched and lashed to the crossplank at the elbows, the uprights bound to their waists. This was intended to encourage good posture. They walked like scarecrows through the market. They were respected by the illiterate. Women would twine flowers into their hand-bindings, ululating toothless invocations for successful voice-making. The master insisted that the crosses not be removed during the first three years of training, except to sleep. Craving further discipline, Johann refused to let his mother untie the cords in the twilight. He placed the tail of his cross on the upper oven ledge and fell asleep, balanced on the compass point of his body, humming figured bass into the coals, which glowed orange-red like illuminated letters in the margins of holy books. His body was like a primed canvas in a stretcher.

The master set them to work in his cherry orchards at harvest time. They were instructed to pick the fruit with gentle fingers. He suggested that the wooden and ivory keys were fruits as well, each with a fine and fragile skin. If this skin were broken the note would spill out of its time. The young Johann Sebastian kept this idea close to his heart. He dreamt of staining his manuscripts with the juice of cherries. He began to think that the spilling of notes could in itself be measured. So began his work in intricate syncopation.

Johann was an ideal student, always asking for more punishment. In the final test of the three-year initiation, the students were forced to sit naked on the bench, balancing twenty-pound grain-scale weights on each shoulder. They were birched every hour for seventy-two hours for good measure, and bullwhipped if they slouched. In his fervour, Johann asked one of his twelve sisters (who, incidentally, was named Veronica) to spoonfeed him wormwood throughout the ordeal. It was then that he hallucinated in counter-tenor, the voice of his Passion narratives...

(...One night I dreamt I was bound to my bench... actually a saddlehorse bristling with iron spikes... music made it rock... beautiful counterpoints of hemiola and french ornamentation... my bag and asshole ripping to shreds... grace notes twiddled by the rhinestoned fingers of fat eunuch professors... my audience was a sallow-faced Bishop, a serpent writhing on his sceptre, nodding the slow nod of one seeing yet another puzzle-piece slide into the jigsaw of some deep theological truth, his skirts bounced by the head of someone sucking him off... and up comes a young nun with syphilis scars for breath... he nods... she disappears... he nods... she gurgles... he nods... she gurgles... he grimaces... I buck... she chokes... he nods... she redoubles her efforts... he indicates his orgasm by scrunging up his lips like the end of a sausage casing... his invisible spunk, smelling of cabbage and frankincense, timed to the V - IV Deceptive Cadence of the Munich School... da Capo al signo... ja ja, all my nightmares are the stolen memories of historical tortures... — I woke up in the music library. Sheets of Brahms and Schubert lay weeping on the floor. Sheets of Mozart tried to comfort them with Punch & Judy skits from the shelves.)

I was always mesmerized that notes could be played with the feet. I imagined the ground into a huge organic pedal-board. Every foothold was a lever connected to a pipe on the other side of the world. Every step sounded a tone. Rotting leaves played flutes. Sewer grates played leaden principles. Sounds of various stringed instruments as I padded through wheat fields. I left no footprints, only echoes. To kneel was to play four notes at once. To kneel with the hands on the earth as when receiving sex from behind was to play six notes. — If I ever have a child I will teach her to tell herself a magical lie much like this one, so she too will be able to animate the lifeless world according to the random steps of her own insomniac dance.

Music, like the sky, is amoral.

My lessons took place in the school auditorium. The afternoon sun seeped into the hospital beige paint. There was a portrait of a dead cardinal over the organ console. A letter of praise for the school from Mother Teresa beside an over-exposed picture of her rotting apple core face, the portrait complemented by a blotch of damprot on the opposite wall. Various missives of encouragement from Rome encouraging the school to continue its vocation of holy music. A papyrus fragment of the letter written by St. Augustine about the singer being the one who prays twice. An oak case with filthy glass revealing a rusted reliquary and several track and field trophies from the turn of the century. (Incidentally, beloved, these details have only been resurrected by squinting at archival photoplates, in which I've ignored the controlling images of elderly teachers and priests and nuns smiling and congratulating each other on another year of chastity and righteousness and ruthlessly scavenged for the Subtexts of Sorrow. I am interested in arrangements of dust, what paint has chipped where. I peer beyond the frames, looking for my soul. — I have worked from photographs because I cannot remember ever having seen anything directly in that room. I was always looking at music; music always pointed into space. My eyes were never focused. My sunspotted devotion kept me from seeing anything closer to my body than Orion. —This is also why I never spoke in complete sentences, and the comma was my secret sign to invite the dark angel in to finish my

)

thoughts.

The organ on which I was taught was installed during the war. Soldiers sleeping in cots in the makeshift auditorium-barracks would be roused with stirring hymns about blood. The ivory keys were chipped and cracked, many of the voice-knobs were missing. (Perhaps damaged by protestants avenging an incident in southern Germany in 1531, in which a drunken Catholic congregation stormed a neighbouring Lutheran church and stole every C-note from the organ, thus crippling the next morning's rendition of "A Mighty Fortress." They ran yelling through the sleeping enemy's fields, using a four-foot flute to bludgeon the screaming protestant sheep until the turf was slippery with blood.*) The pipes were enclosed behind the stage, plastered in behind the thin walls of tiny rooms furnished with bunk beds with rotting mattresses for the two boarders, the orphans. During the day these were used as sickbeds. The boarders were often tucked in with the smell of barf hanging in the room. I would often complain of headaches during mathematics, and be excused to go in and lie down beside the pipes, and have the organ scholar unwittingly play me into a sleep beyond calculus. I have never seen as much light as when I closed my eyes during those hours. Just as white contains all colours, silence contains all sound.

My organ teacher had been a virtuoso and a cocaine addict as a young man. He was thirty-five, had no children and cared for an invalid mother — highly volatile, exquisitely repressed... As a boy he studied in Oxford under a severe old queen who wore silk cravats and fellated him at the end of every lesson. The boy stood at attention in a musty corner of the choir loft while the head of neatly coifed silver hair bobbed at his belt level. He grabbed at the ears of marble gargoyles and clenched his eyes against candle and fresco when the sucking pulled his hips off balance. The master admonished him for this compensatory technique, elegantly removing the tiny penis from his mouth as though it were an ivory cigarette holder: MM MM-HMN SHMACKPTOO HMN M-MOST DISAPPOINTING. YOUR HANDS MUST BE FREE TO PLAY, MY BOY. IT IS YOUR SPINE WHICH MUST CONTROL YOUR BALANCE, AND IF YOU THINK THAT THIS IS UNBALANCING, JUST WAIT UNTIL YOU LEARN MENDELSSOHN... NOW, BE A GOOD BOY AND CUM INTO MY MOUTH. — The boy obliged, making no sound, mesmerized by the extreme dignity of the scene, biting his lip. — His orgasm

---

* as reported in *Christe's Horrore at Popishe Debaucherie*, a pamphlet published anonymously in London, 1538.

was intimately connected to the calm pain of the sanctuary lamp glowing red behind its shade of clouded glass.

   This boy grew up and I began my studies under him and his pre-scriptions of methadone and valium. My pedagogical hierarchy throbbed towards completion. Its powers arranged themselves as follows:

Veronica, my sister (cf. novel)
|
19th Century Orthodox Catholic Rhetoric
|
Dead Cardinals Laid In State,
Their Odours Masked by Toilet Fresheners
|
Holy Cards And Leather Straps
|
Dead Languages
|
Sacred Music Written In Monasteries
Wiped Out By Plague
|
Visions Of Martyrs Experienced In
Physical Trauma Such As Rectal Tearing
|
Great Organists Of History Who Made Kings Smile
|
My Teacher's Memory
|
My Teacher's Invalid Mother
|
My Teacher's Shrink (Freudian)
|
My Teacher's Neuro-Stimulants
|
My Teacher's Marlboro Breath
|

My Teacher's Prematurely Rasping Voice

|

My Teacher's Insectoid Fingers

|

My Teacher's Dilated Pupils Set Into Encrusted Eyelids

|

My Fear Of My Teacher's Lust

|

My Envisioning Of My Teacher's Cockhole Bleeding

|

My Fear Of Urinating In Anxiety

|

God (not essential to this schema)

|

My Secret Private Prayers

|

My Body.

He had his bad days. — HOW CAN I DO ANYTHING WITH A LITTLE JERK WHO DOESN'T PRACTICE but I did SOUNDS LIKE NOT FUCKIN ENOUGH NOW HOW MANY HOURS A DAY about two TWO? TWO? YOU PRACTICE TWO HOURS? HOW CAN WE ACCOMPLISH ANYTHING HERE YOU LITTLE WANKER DO YOU HAVE ANY CLUE HOW MUCH I WAS AT IT AT YOUR AGE no BECAUSE I WASN'T WILL- ING TO WASTE MY TALENT TO TO TO JUST THROW MYSELF AWAY? DO YOU KNOW no DO YOU? no NO WHAT? no sir EIGHT FUCKIN HOURS A DAY YEAH IN THAT CATHEDRAL Y' KNOW THEY DIDN'T HEAT THE GODDAMN PLACE THEN AND THAT WAS ONLY TWENTY YEARS AGO I HAD TO CUT THE FINGERS OUT OF MY GLOVES AND ONE LITTLE PEANUT BUTTER SAMWICH FOR LUNCH AND THE DEACON DIDN'T LET ME TURN ON THE LAMP AT NIGHT TO SAVE ELECTRICITY I LEARNED THE WHOLE ORGELBUCHLEIN BY THE LIGHT OF A KEROSENE LAMP

AND EVERYTHING HAD TO BE PERFECT FOR MONDAY
MORNING CAUSE IF MY TEACHER WASN'T HAPPY WITH
ME I HAD TO CLEAN THE BIRD SHIT OUTTA THE
PIPES AND THEN KNEEL THE REST OF THE DAY IN
THE YARD IN THE FUCKIN SNOW WHAT DO YOU THINK
THIS IS FUCKIN DAYCARE SHIT YOU MAKE ME SICK
I'D RATHER LISSEN TO SKELETONS FUCKING ON A
TIN ROOF OR EVEN SOME CIPHERS* WOULD BE A WEL-
COME CHANGE NOW YOU WANNA KNOW HOW TO PLAY A
FUGUE YOU WANNA LEARN TO PLAY A FUGUE ANSWER
ME yeah WHAT? yes sir I'LL TELL YA HOW TO PLAY A
FUCKIN FUGUE LISSEN TO ME NOW HAVE YOU EVER
QUARTERED YOUR BRAIN AND MADE THE SLICED
PIECES TALK TO EACH OTHER, IDIOT? THAT'S WHAT
THE ORGAN IS LIKE YOU IDIOT THAT'S WHAT A
FUGUE IS ABOUT YOU IDIOT AND REMEMBER THAT
FUGUE MEANS ESCAPE BUT THERE'S NO FUCKIN
ESCAPE FROM A FUGUE OR FROM HARD FUCKIN WORK
— After screaming away twelve minutes of a forty-five
minute lesson while rendering my music illegible with
snaky leaden scars, he would tell me to continue playing,
reach into his jacket pocket to retrieve orange labelled
bottles and retreat behind the stage curtains to fall asleep

---

* "Ciphering" — the sounding of an organ pipe without a key being
depressed, due to mechanical fault or damage. Not to be confused with
"running," i.e. the leaking of wind from one groove or channel to another, audible only when a neighbouring key is depressed. Common reasons
for ciphering will be found in a faulty pallet (dust preventing full closure,
a pallet being dislodged, warped, damp or catching on guide pins), pallet
spring (out of position, too weak, broken), action (tight or entangling
tracker, damaged backfall, jammed, bent or rusty pull-down), slider
(loose, warped), or key (warped, stuck) and, in non-mechanical actions,
failures at various critical points (contacts, relays, key springs, inert pneu-
matics, etc). It seems to me that a cipher is the first indication of decen-
tralized intelligence within the organ. From the listed examples, we see
that the ciphering pipe wins its detachment from the machine's sonic
autocracy through self-mutilation. I want to be a cipher. Singing because
I'm damaged, because I've damaged myself.

in a bottom bunk. Sometimes I was interested in the work at hand, and continued playing, uncorrected, until the time was up. Sometimes I stopped playing altogether, and spent the rest of the lesson staring at the dead Bishop's cold eyes of silver gelatin. The sagging flesh under his chin dripped like seal-tallow into fronds of yellowed lace.

Once I played straight through to the end of the lesson, watching my time of instruction come to an end through the reflection of the clock onto a window that looked out over a detox centre (— which was an organ in its own right, divisions of reedy delusion and schizoid *fourniture* blown by the calm sterilized wind of fluorescence and bed-straps). In reflection, the clock ran backwards. — Just as John Cage's 3' 44" comes to an end after three minutes and forty-four seconds, time ran out on the lesson. — I peeked around the curtain to wake my teacher up. His sleeping body was ashen, harped by the barred shadows of fire escapes. Corroding bedsprings dangled over him like carillon wire. His trousers bunched around his thighs. Holding his cock like a worm in his right hand. Threads of cum across his stomach in a milky web. His eyes opened and fixed upon me. He didn't move. I fled to the yard and threw up against the wall.

I hadn't gone back to collect my music. It was delivered to me in the following class, with an innocent note from him listing my assignments for the next lesson. I found I couldn't open the books to practise that week, disgusted at the idea that the pages were writhing with his sperm, that the music was being rewritten by his seed, that the combination of ancient melodies and his madness would give me a horrendous disease localized in my fingertips, and I would no longer have any control over my playing.

Ten thousand hours of hypnotizing myself with my own fingers. After seven years, I was good enough for the monsignor to schedule me into the cathedral roster of organists. Holy Week, 1988. I had time for one lesson on the cathedral instrument in the eyeless vacancy of an early March afternoon.

Heaven wore a blue FOR RENT sign. My teacher secured rehearsal space for me between the hour of confession and the hour of benediction. I entered the neo-gothic vestibule and splashed my hand in the lavabo. I licked the holy-water from my fingers. The door to the choir loft open, the passageway lit by a single caged bulb. I ascended the spiral-staircase-cathedral-rectal-tract quietly, expecting Him to be waiting for me above, perhaps asleep on a choir bench. He wasn't there. It was like getting stood up by a confessor, left standing in the rain with a bouquet of wrong-doings. I decided to begin playing without him. I went to the ancient fuse-box, which bristled with frayed copper. I threw the switch and waited for the great inhalation of that magnificent machine.

The coroner sat in his crumpled Burbery at our kitchen table, stroking the dent in his Homburg like it was the fontanelle of a stillbirth. He informed our pale and shivering mother that when I turned on the instrument, surging beads of electricity flowed from the Don River Hydro Plant into the power line nailed to the cathedral wall in snaking loops around the bas-reliefs of martyrs and shot up into the fusebox and were dispersed, little fire ants, to various worksites, the most important of which was the blower mechanism for the windchest. The blades of the fan began to turn, and their cut steel edges bit slowly into a strange heavy rope that ran from a tether below the fan-teeth to a pulley at the top of the carillon tower, then down to where it split into two strands with a two-by-four knotted between the ends like a homemade swing in a summer yard. On this swing stood my teacher, his thin body naked and blue and convulsed with cold and heroin and desire, pulling furiously at his cock. His facial description would be presented here if he had not been wearing a black leather mask with studs that gleamed like Gregorian neums in photo-negative. Around his neck was a noose made from the end of a bell-rope. The fan, rubbing and biting against the twine, didn't produce any air flow. I drew a voice, pressed a key, and the instrument sighed mournfully. — The world paused. In Rome, a restorer toothbrushed away some candle-grime over God's Sistine Chapel eye to reveal an eyebrow of Groucho Marx proportion... — Finally, the fan broke through the rope, the air rushed into the wooden belly, the platform gave way, his body plunged, his hand quickened as his lungs emptied, and he ejaculated into the shaft with a strangled cry. The enormous bell rang and snapped his writhing body skywards with its rebound, his skull striking the rim and splitting in the leather mask, as I, filled with excitement, began to play, all of my voices now freed by the unseen gusts of wind. (The theorists call this phenomenon auto-erotic asphyxiation. This suggests that he desired himself. What bullshit. Can they really think that the desperate get off on themselves? What a happy world it would be if this were true.)

The sudden bell-ringing confused me. I stopped playing and climbed the steps to the carillon shaft, expecting Our Father to be pulling the ropes off cue, pissed and tottering. He wasn't there. I gazed down the shaft. The body of my teacher bounced in its bonds like a cat toy in the hand of an epileptic child. Blood ran down his chest and hips and thighs from his opened skull still hidden by the mask. Blood dripped from his glans. The bell rang and he bobbed and it rang and he bobbed and I knew he would ring that bell forever, because I finally understood the solution to the essential problem of mechanics: that only suicide is a perpetual motion machine... only suicide involves no loss of energy. And every body must have its cadenza, like the wings of birds twitching in death, playing out that final memory of flight. — I gathered my music, turned off the blower, descended the staircase, and sat down on a bench across the street in the falling dusk. I listened to the ringing become slower and fainter until my teacher's life was nothing but a pale blue echo playing through the empty streets.

There is a delightful bit of information from the renaissance period that may or may not be appropriate here, concerning what makes things work, what lives and dies hidden. Like Da Vinci says about impetus: "*...[it is] a power transmitted from the mover to the movable thing, and maintained by the wave of the air within the air which this mover produces; and this arises from the vacuum and returns to it...*" As we've just seen, electricity was an essential ingredient in the rigged suicide of my Hero, the power surge that set the fan into motion and the blades against the twine. This fan is meant to create steady wind pressure. It is the contemporary version of the ancient bellows-mechanism, which, until the mid-nineteenth century, was operated manually, sometimes with a pair of step-bellows that a hired serf would foot-pump in an eternal climb towards nothing. (— And who will say whether he was more connected to the product of his labour than the yuppie who spends hour after hour on the Stairmaster in the spa listening to Top 40 radio on his Walkman?)

Before the step-bellow, the organ got its wind by more insidious means. A two-headed pipe was fixed upright in a nearby creek. The shorter end drew in water, the pressure of which sucked air through the higher end, which ascended above the water level. Water and air were separated on the bank by a series of screens, and the air flowed through leaden pipes into the church. Of course, rainfall, drought, and irregular tidal factors made the flow of air inconsistent, necessitating a regulating mechanism. Giant lambskin bladders were enclosed in the windchests beneath the instrument to hold the air. Its flow, then, had to be pushed towards the pipes evenly. How fortunate that violent times yielded such a rich harvest of orphans for just such a purpose! Yes, little boys and girls were locked into these chests and forced to walk on the bladder like dancing monkeys, keeping it pressed below a certain level marked with scarlet paint. Just as bigger text files require more memory, faster and more intricate music required those little ragbound feet to pick up the pace. And they had definite incentive to continue, despite probable hunger and exhaustion, for if they paused, the river would continue to flow, the pipes would continue to draw air, the bladder would continue to fill, the collapsed child would be crushed against the ceiling of the chest, while, in the church, the recessional hymn would cut out in the middle of the last verse for lack of wind. Better to keep running. I have often romantically thought of myself as that child, forced to press my body against a lung full of words that fills itself from some unnameable source governed by *nature,* and I have to keep running, stomping on that lung to keep it from crushing me against the ceiling of a room that only I have seen... almost hearing the music from the other side... such pure amoral diapasons...

But perhaps there is an even more suitable analogy for our nightmare — one that includes you explicitly, beloved reader. When a river wasn't handy, the air had to be manipulated in a hermetically sealed system. Two bladders were required, each housed in its own case, connected by a t-pipe leading up to the pipe-bed. Two urchins were required in this system, one running on one bladder until half of its air was in the opposite bladder, and then the other running, to force it back. The resulting suction drew in a third stream of air from the outside. As we may imagine, a high degree of coordination was required to keep everything safely operating, for if one of the two children (obviously, I imagine that they were often siblings) didn't start running in time, he or she would be crushed. But perhaps it was a safer environment than the one previously mentioned, because they could keep each other company in their slavery, much like a driver will ask the navigator to keep talking on late-night excursions. — So it is with you and I, dear reader, each of us running madly in the hidden rooms of a demonic machine, passing centuries of stale air and words back and forth, each proceeding on blind faith that the other both exists and cares enough not to become negligent and therefore murderous. And we too can vaguely hear the music that is produced on the other side of the church wall, which is beginning more and more to ressemble the cover of a book.

The only question left for us is: who is playing this Instrument, and why? Let's just say it's the Player. Perhaps the Player is performing entrance marches for cosmic weddings. Perhaps it is a dirge drawing the fibreglass coffins out into the searing u.v. rays, which we barely remember having ever felt on our faces, caged as we have been. Perhaps the Player has no audience at all, and is simply lazily practising for some future recital. Or perhaps... the Player is doing nothing at all... because the pipes were stolen long ago by epistemological bandits... the music we think we are hearing is but the echo of some lost song trapped in the cabinet with us.... The Player balances on the bench, receiving the soundless gust on Its face... bringing the vaguest remembrance... a story of beginnings... Broken Wind over Fetid Waters...

Let me now openly confess that this novel has been entirely financed by **THE ROMAN CATHOLIC CHURCH**, through virtue of my job as a church organist. My pastor ignores me. — I write on the grey weekdays from which the Sabbath steals its scraps of light, and I study the music for upcoming feast days by candlelight and hash haze. The melodies always become more complicated, sometimes based on the amount I drink, sometimes on the amount I pray. My apartment walls are turning brown.

I steal money and language and image from the Church. I invest these talents in fiction stocks. If they turn over empty I will be totally merciless, and steal from the poor-boxes too. My sister taught me to feel no guilt about such theft. For as Klaus Shreiner tells us: "medieval monks involved in the act of stealing relics to grace their shrines were always able to cite abundant precedents from the Old Testament in which the divine will was effected through lying, stealing, trickery, and other such means."

Things would have been different if I'd grown up learning to play the violin. I would have nestled the strings against my neck. I would have walked across the tundra of my childhood with the instrument, playing, playing as a single bead of phosphorous light moving through the fault-lines of the sea, events swimming past me like translucent fish, all the dead bodies floating as gently as my own. — I couldn't carry the organ with me from shrine to shrine. It was bolted to the floor like an electric chair. — With a violin, I could have been a gypsy for God. I could have carried the infinite possibilities of singular melody, and people would have known me by whatever name I painted on its rosewood neck. I would have made the strings say the word "I", and I would have been sure as to whom that word referred. Violins compress the lonely ego into a raindrop that can describe its own falling and never worry about not being heard. Organs disperse the ego over countless times and bodies, which are subsequently brainwashed into singing choruses for dead audiences. (Systems devouring components, bodies noosed by the bootstrap theories of the corporate.) — Sister, this is my letter to you, so for now I will indulge in the lie of my control. I see this, my first-person voice, as a violin, inherited from you. Its four strings were supposed to wear the names of Faith, Hope, Love and Charity, for the violin-maker was a Child of God. I was given the alphabet for a bow to draw across these virtues and send prayers jackknifing into heaven.

The original strings broke when you left, Veronica. Out of weakness I replaced them with Lust, Disease, Cynicism and Fear. The alphabet bow has somehow remained intact.

The Bishop likes me. He lets me use his condo in New Toronto, overlooking the lake. There are silk sheets on the queen-size bed. I bet he has great fun examining his pimply ass in the ceiling mirrors as it pumps away over some shamed-but-loving-it housewife... — O how I wish that you could look from my window with me now. The lake ripples with the unaddressed letters of the wind. Between my window and the water there is a breakwater of rock assembling itself upwards into a stone wall which dirty-faced children turn into a castle turret on Sundays, shooting arrows of high-pitched screams into watery beasts with the longbows of impossibly synapsed imaginations, and after the stone wall there is a boardwalk of decaying concrete, planted with a single bench built to the same dimensions of the organ, and beside this lonely bench smeared with guano and seeping out the ass-warmth of Sunday-walking widowers who gazed out into the swirling instrument looking for that music stand in the mist, and, failing to find it, left for the pub... Beside this lonely bench stands a trash can.

And lo, here comes the garbage man, pushing a wooden cart with a shovel leaned up inside it for picking up dogshit. He is old and thin with a face like a rat. He stops the cart beside the bin, looks out to the waves, reaches a palsied hand into a greasy pocket, removes a tin flask and swigs a toast to the ambiguous joy of water and effluent. He caps the flask, and peers into the bin. He is employed by the city to do its shitwork, much like me, employed by the church, drinking on the sly between orthodox renditions of hymns scavenged from stinking crypts, going unnoticed by the clergy even when kneeling in front of grottoes and lighting candles for my dead. He rustles through the trash, keeping the interesting things, note-books, photographs, sanitary pads whose brown stains resemble impressionist maps of Palestine. He tucks them into his pockets — I, too, sift garbage, perhaps not so dis-criminately. — He moves on, suddenly losing interest in hanging around for me to finish my meditation. I can't blame him.

The garbage man by the bench by the sea reminds me of a certain lover. Having failed so many times at describing her beauty, I will simply describe what she does, by saying this. She too is a scavenger, she too stops to look out at the sea. — I watch her sit down on the bench, which is like a single ice-chair on a glacier to which she's been lashed and then whipped by a past concurrent to mine. Her back is perfectly straight, having learned something about balancing between a universe that doesn't want her and the HUNGRY PIT. She keeps her eyes fixed on the horizon. — Somewhere, the distance between her and her desire has vanished.

Sometimes when I practised late at the Cathedral, I brought toys with me. I used to pause my pedal scales and climb down from the loft, my Evel Kneivel doll plus motorcycle and launch-crank under my arm. I'd set Evel up at the bottom of the main aisle and start cranking. The inertia-motor of the cycle whined like an air raid siren. The saints watched from their windows as Evel popped a 200-foot wheelie all the way to a cool altar-bottom spin-out. Once I made a sheet-music ramp for him on the altar steps. Evel flew through the air and bonged against the tabernacle door.

shofar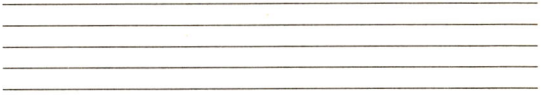

bohdraín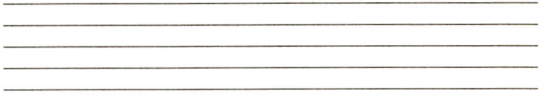

singsing saw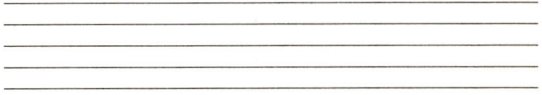

tabla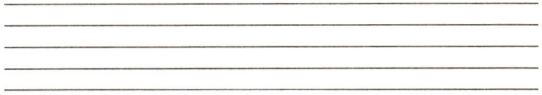

continuo
(vox humana)

shakuhachi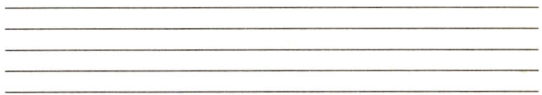

fender
(with distortion + wa-wa)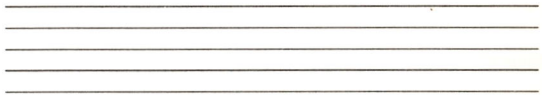

dung chen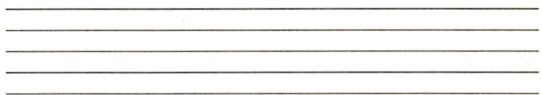

washtub bass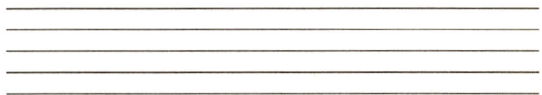

64.

Veronica, I have been writing these true things for sixty-four days from the same room. I ask for no remuneration. Writing is not a profession any more than bleeding is. Those who do it for money are much bigger liars than I. That's why they get hired by news agencies. — The sky is bloated with sky-descriptions, signifying a general cultural unwillingness to look at the immediate materiality of, say, our hands. — My hands… My hands are my hands.

I learned to type in a class taught by a nun. No secular textbooks were allowed. The exercises were taken from prayers.

Sister Evangelica barked out the letters and directions for arranging the prayer on the page:

CAP Hail SPACECAP Mary COMMASPACE full RETURN
of SPACE grace COMMASPACE the SPACECAP Lord RETURN
is SPACE with SPACE thee PERIODSPACERETURN
CAP Blessed SPACE art SPACE thou SPACE among RETURN
women COMMASPACE and SPACE blessed SPACE is RETURN
the SPACE fruit SPACE of SPACE thy SPACE womb RETURN
CAP Jesus PERIODSPACESPACECAP Holy RETURN
CAP Mary COMMASPACECAP Mother SPACE of RETURN
CAP God COMMASPACE pray SPACE for SPACE us RETURN
sinners COMMASPACE now SPACE and SPACE at RETURN
the SPACE hour SPACE of SPACE our RETURN
death PERIODRETURNTWICE

By the end of that year the opening exercise of each typing class was the every-letter-in-the-alphabet drill: Saint Zoe sang that Jesus leaps down from the crucifix whenever the martyrs beckon the quick to love.

The final exam consisted of typing out the entire mass in Latin, with the correct capitalization and spacing, again while looking only at the crucifix. Sister saying Remember, if one letter is out of place, it is not a mass. As the time wound out and my mistakes became more frequent I wondered whether a whole room full of boys with hard-ons and girls with sweating backs typing out HOC EST CORPUM MEUM could make something happen in another part of the world, or even here, the newsprint with fuzzy lettering transubstantiating into silk, leathered skin, the perfect veil.

(— I saw a deaf woman this morning talking to herself in sign language. She was so graceful. *She was whispering to me: This is what typing is, dear.* Her hearing aids shone like snails.)

65.

i have   discovered through   the   waltz   of   desiccation that i cannot   create the world. that sparrow   . that goddamned   sun   and   the   brilliant day paying   me no   heed   .   the sun is   incongruent   with my   wormhole heart . shreds of   a wedding dress . hosannas sleeping   on the pasty tongue . the   world continues   in spite of hope and those believed to be without hope . the   incongruent living planet   . thanatos is this : desire   for symmetry.   thanatos and symmetry alike are superfluous con- structs . shreds of a   phenomenological wedding   dress waiting   for transcription so white

(what follows are scribbles even I can't read, sister.)

66.

Once there was a man who decided to devote his life to making his headstone. He began his education in carving by running his fin through still bodies of water. The ripples moved over the submerged continents to the ends of the world, colliding at the opposite pole. This was good. He walked out of the sea on his separated tail and knelt to push his new fingers across the sand, nudging the trilo-bites. He drew a rudimentary alphabet and sat back to watch the ebb carry it away to underwater dictionaries. This was good. Then he stepped back onto the higher ground of the beach and came upon a piece of driftwood vaguely resembling a swan. It was soft with water and rot, and he was able to form the neck and wings with his hands. The soft slivers bent in under his nails. When he had finished, he sat with the swan for many months, watching the worms eat it from inside. Its wooden spine cracked. This was good in his heart, which was forming to human completion around its own shimmering parasites.

He was pleased with what he had learned, and turned to enter the forest. In a clearing he came upon two monoliths of white marble. He said *One of these will be my headstone, it will mark where I fall. My family will set it over my body, and it will be my sign.* A trumpet seared its note over the walled city in the distance.

He dragged the stones home on a sled, one in the morn-ing, one in the evening, cords lashed around his shoulders. He set them in a room in the centre of his house. He climbed to the roof and tore away the thatch. The light and rain would bathe and illuminate his labour.

He began to carve one of the slabs into an image of him-self. He began to form the head, the brow. Dust fell upon his arms, and the night dew pressed it into his skin. His hand, though softened by water and sand and wood, was harsh and impatient. His fury at his inaccuracies flashed through the chisel. He gouged out an eye for the imperfec-

tions of its eyelid. The stone dwindled under his flashing
rage, until he was working himself in miniature. He soon
found himself looking at white dust on an earthen floor.
The rain came through and filled the ruts, turned milky
with the dust, and flowed away. He looked at what he had
come to. Even this was good, because he could begin
again, knowing more about ignorance.

Time passed. One of his daughters was bought by a
neighbouring tribe. Another died in childbirth at the same
moment that her starving husband drank the blood of a
fellow sailor on a galleon bound for China. Factories melted copper. A son donned a steel helmet and waded
through trenches among bits of scorched metal. Another
sat in a small room for years, gazing blindly at the sky
through a window lined with vials of white powder.
Electricity brought him music from towers which had
replaced trees on distant mountains. The man's wife
learned to read, and left him to attend to her long-sub-
merged needs. He said *I will begin again. These hands are
gentler now with no one needing them. There is nothing left for
me to do except to complete the work I began years ago.*

And so he began to work with the second stone, starting
this time from the vertebrae. The stone had been polished
by centuries of rain and frozen air. Very little of the house
remained around him. He would fall into sleep with the
chisel in his hand and his arm around the stony foot, his
mouth open to the stars. He was awoken periodically by
airplanes passing over.

His hand was gentler now. He knew the patience of one
whose grave lies open and waiting, every chisel-tap guided
by wisdom and empathy. He carved every scar — visible
and invisible — into the stone. Life transferred touch by
touch from one body to another. He resided in deep prayer
before every cut, asking *What is the truth of that line, that
depth, the precise way I felt at that moment?* He prayed in the
perfect voice of a child, ranging innocently through
octaves of wonder. His mind was as a pitcher of whale bone

set to rest under a waterfall. — In the evenings he circled his ruined house, his bare feet in the ash. The blue glow of television palled the brokenwalled city in the distance.

As the headless statue watched over him with unformed eyes, he covered his face and scalp with aloes, leaving two holes through which to breathe. He made a mould of his skull with plaster. He sat motionless for three days until it had dried, impervious to the distant clamour. Satisfied that the plaster was dry, he raised his chisel and touched its tip to the forehead of the mask. With a single blow the cast split through its centre. The chisel grazed his brow. Blood trickled into his eye. The two halves fell to the earth. He washed the dusty aloe from his eyes, picked up the pieces, and reassembled them, fixing them with epoxy. He spent the next several days with his hands inside the mold, his fingertips reading the brailled imprint of his nape, brow, ear to the inner canal, and cranium. He used an ultrasound gun to produce a perfect electronic image of the texture, which he read and studied from a magenta screen. He knew he could begin to work when he dreamt that he was walking barefoot on the moon, and the moon was his skull, and the pads of his feet recognized every mound and crevice before stepping. He took up his chisel.

When he completed the head he began to fashion the face, working from the mirror of his memory, which was as a glass sheer-polished by those fine sands of change that ran through his fingers so long ago. From a block of waste removed from the side of the figure, he whittled seventy teardrops of stone, and strung them into an abacus-frame. He then began to catalogue the tears of his life from his precise journal entries, counting each one. The stone beads clicked like insects under his wizened fingers. When he had finished, he entered the final figure into his computer, along with the variables of his age, living altitude, elemental exposure and environmental decay. To these numbers he applied a calculus that would accurately produce the scarred trajectories of his face in pixilated lines.

He printed out the resulting parabolae with lasers, amassing thousands of sketches to precede the first touch on the stone that was to become his cheek. He thought of his eyes as containing everything and nothing, producing the empty artifacts of inscription and retaining the ability to read. — The earth beneath him warmed with radioactive springs. Overhead, the tails of comets replaced themselves with the shooting fire of afterburners ascending, wayward to celestial loss.

On the last day of the world, he poised his hand for the last touch of the chisel. He looked to earth and to heaven for guidance, inclining his head to hear words of direction that did not come. There was no sign. Standing on his arbitrary aesthetic precipice, he inhaled the waning light, and brought the gleaming edge to the stone. He brought the mallet down, removing the last fragment that stood between his body and what he was making himself to be. The chip fell to the ground, rested a moment, and then entered the earth, which closed over the motionless burrowing, the seed of a final imperfection. He felt ignorant again.

He raised his eyes over the stone body before him, straining to see the details by the red dusk. Foot, leg, genitals, abdomen, chest, arm, shoulder, neck. He was the last human at the end of the world, and this was good, and this was passing. The stone stood solid against the night. He began to shake at the sight, overcome by the grief and joy of his image, made by one who had disappeared in the process of creating it. He was unable to weep, for there would be no time to add evidence of new tears to the stone.

He reeled into the black, pulled by an unseen hand. He died, observed.

— A Parable by GOD

67.

Little brother, you're like St. Francis who went out into the gypsy quarter of Assisi, his habit stuffed with communion bread. He handed the unleavened loaves into leprous hands and smiled like a postcard. Those who were starving exulted in their brief reprise. St. Francis felt good. He felt so good about himself that he looked down into his cloak, and the loaves of bread had turned to roses. He undid his belt and the roses gushed forward as if from a splitting wine cask. Then he began to bleed.

It was nice, but a bit romantic. The world was suspicious. The world used the voice of the city. The city used the voice of the ghetto. The ghetto used the voice of the gypsies. The gypsies used the voice of a little girl who said *that is very beautiful, dom francis, but my brothers and i will still be hungry tomorrow.* But St. Francis was mesmerized by the wonders of his own body and ignored her plaintive voice, thinking of how he would show this miracle to his beloved ravens, to his pretty doves, to his cute swallows, to those dumb creatures who ask so little.

68.

This novel is about the author carving himself up so he can have friends to play hide-and-seek with. He calls one of his amputations "Veronica".

*

---

* Ex-postulate # 1: Postmodernism is like sixty-nining the foetal corpse of your twin in a dune of tv snow.

69.

VERONICA VERONICA VERONICA VERONICA VERONICA
VERONICA VERONICA VERONICA VERONICA VERONICA
VERONICA VERONICA VERONICA VERONICA VERONICA
VERONICA VERONICA VERONICA VERONICA VERONICA
VERONICA VERONICA VERONICA VERONICA VERONICA
VERONICA VERONICA VERONICA VERONICA VERONICA
VERONICA VERONICA VERONICA VERONICA VERONICA
VERONICA VERONICA VERONICA VERONICA VERONICA
VERONICA VERONICA VERONICA VERONICA VERONICA
VERONICA VERONICA VERONICA VERONICA YOUR NAME
IS THE BEGINNING OF A SELF-WRITING ALPHABET.
THIS IS THE INSOMNIA OF THE NEW FACE IN LOVE.
LET'S QUARRY THE HEART. LET'S DRINK SPIKENARD
MIXED WITH WATER. LET'S FORGET OURSELVES IN
THE HALF LIGHT CALLED ADRENALINE. WHEN APART,
WE FALL ASLEEP IN OUR CLOTHES. WHEN APART, WE
THROW OURSELVES FROM WINDOWS ALMOST HIGH
ENOUGH TO KILL. THE UGLY MUSIC OF BREATHING.
THE SPONTANEOUS TRADITION, MAKING ITSELF OVER
WITH RED CLAY. BALCONIES OF THE WORLD, PLEASE
HEAR US THROUGH THE NOVEMBER AIR. MARROW OF
OUR MARROW. CELL OF OUR CELL. FATIGUE AND
DEHYDRATION. CONSUMMATED ELEMENTS. LOVE HAS
AN ILLEGIBLE PERIODIC TABLE. TWISTING THE
BLOODLINE INTO A CROWN OF SOFTEST THORN. LIFE
DRAWING IN THE DARK. ISOLATION CHAMBER WHERE
THE MIND TUNES ITS STRINGS. WE HAND OUR
CLAUSTROPHOBIA BACK AND FORTH LIKE A DOVE IN
SLOW AND TENDER PERISHING. YOUR NAME IS THE
SOUND WHERE THE CITIES OF THE WORLD LOSE
THEIR PSEUDONYMS AND THE SAINTS SLEEP IN
RAILWAY TOILET STALLS. WHERE THE PLUMBING
STARTS TO LEAK. WHERE THE VESSELS WEAR THEIR
HAIRLINE FRACTURES LIKE THE PAINT AROUND OUR
EYES. WHERE THE KILN WEEPS ITS ASBESTOS INTO

OUR PALMS, SEARING ALL TIMELINES. YOUR NAME IS WHERE THE SEWERS KISS THE AIR. WHERE WE ASK WHERE ARE WE, AND NEVER FIND OUT, BECAUSE WE HAVE MOVED SINCE THE ASKING. WHERE THE SIX YEAR OLD USES A CHICKEN BONE TO WRITE CALLIGRAPHY. WHERE THE TWO YEAR OLD STOPS BREATHING IN ITS SLEEP. WHERE THERE IS NO QUESTION ABOUT THE COLOUR OF RAIN, OR WHAT THE MOON IS, OR THE ETHICS OF SUICIDE. WHERE ABERRATION IS THE GRAMMAR OF SMALL AND MIRACULOUS ANIMALS, HUDDLING. WHERE THE ANAPHORA DOES NOT BREAK DOWN, EVEN WHEN APPLIED TO THE GENERATION OF NAMES FOR ALL STARS. WHERE THE WORD PROCESSING PROGRAM SEIZES, REFUSING TO WORK AT ANYTHING EXCEPT ITS OWN TALENT FOR CONCRETE POEMS THAT ACTUALLY BURN WATTS.

O DEAREST LOVE, WEAR THE MASK THAT HAS CHOSEN YOU FOR ITS CARRIER. THAT'S HOW I WILL KNOW YOU.

WEARING OUT THE PRESSES, THE ALPHABET CONTINUES TO PRINT ITSELF, DESIGNING ITS CHARACTERS WITH THE AID OF FRACTAL GENERATORS. STRIPPING THE LANGUAGE TO ITS OWN IDEAS OF GRACE. WHERE SACRAMENT DEVELOPS LIKE A DIALECT AMONG HERB-GATHERING PRIMATES. A FLOWER THAT BLOOMS IN THE CREVICES OF GLACIERS THAT MELT INTO SEROTONIN. A SPORE RELEASED BY AMBER. A PHOTOGRAPH THAT TRAPS MANNA AND CORRODES THE CAMERA LIKE A LEAKING BATTERY. GREEN ACID AMONG THE LENSES AND GEARS. A NOVEL THAT TOUCHES ITSELF IN A MOMENT, AND KNOWS ITS OWN STORY, AND SEEKS TO EXTEND ITS PAGES LIKE A SECOND CORPUS CALLOSUM THROUGH CANCEROUS FOLDS OF TISSUE. A PAINTING THAT PAINTS YOU, SWALLOWING YOUR ANXIETY INTO A NEW ACOUSTIC WITH EVERY BLEED-

ING LINE OF BURNT SIENNA. YOUR NAME IS A
BRUSH MADE FROM THE SOFTEST HAIRS OF YOUR
BODY. PALETTE COMPOSED OF THE EPITHELIUM YOU
HAVE SHED IN THE BRIEF YEARS SINCE THE PLA-
CENTA ENVELOPED YOUR SKULL AND ABDOMEN. YOUR
NAME IS WHAT RECOMPOSES YOU. WHAT SAYS THE
WORD ARTERY, AND MAKES YOUR FACE RECOGNIZABLE
IN ALL MIRRORS. WHAT SAYS THE WORD ALVEOLUS,
AND REMINDS YOU OF THE BEAUTIFUL BINDING OF
YOUR BODY.

*

---

* Ex-postulate # 2: This is a beautiful star in the night sky.

70. THIS NOVEL AS OUT-TAKES FROM A FILM BY INGMAR BERGMAN, b&w, 73min, all-amateur Scandinavian cast, shot on location in a Muskokan forest, mid-January, circa 1930...

A man and a woman are walking through oak and pine. Prayers have chosen to stop themselves. No creature, even in hiding. She has wrapped his scarf around her head, holding it at her throat. They are lit from underneath. This is a winter reflection. The sky sending down its mirrors, remembering nothing about blue. There is a strange light from space, and their feet break the snow. His font of words has frozen, for he has seen trees cradling children that do not move. Her song has left, for in her body she looks on the moon. Someone else will record these things.

Spheres of ice in a brook. A bird's nest fallen. Snow webbing roots that lie bare. A stain that the mind spreads on things, sepia, saying *Remember this*. Their arms touching on the next step. Fatigue supplanted by what is seen. It is late, but they are not tired. An airplane rolls its boom over the next county, and they walk. Snow falls into snow from a branch jostled by a shoulder. If she thinks she is

---

The Lateral Exhaustion of Works and Days

Absence flowed in. Inside the absence, people wanted people or a God to want them. Want gazed at itself in mirrors. Mirrors shattered into glittering fragments.

warm she will not be cold, her mother
told her on the way to church years ago.
If he thinks he is living he will not be
dead, his confessor told him, and he
believed it, though now she shivers. From
time to time they look up from the path as
though distracted by a bird while reading from the same book.

Her eyes approach out of the night. A
tree may fall, a dam may break. She has
stopped shivering. He shifts his weight,
cracking the skull of a frozen
woodthrush underfoot. They do not hear
this, blanketed from themselves. They are
waiting for desire to enter from the
outer dark, although the world is tuned
to itself and has no need for endings. A
small bird does not call out, though
silence is living.
When she was a girl she made snow
angels. When he was a boy he listened to
the old man next door lose his mind while
playing the violin. He also killed insects
by snapping his book shut on summer
nights.

They have reached a lake, an impossible
horizon. Infinity signs carved into the
ice by vanished skaters. Paw prints of an

Fragmented mirrors went opaque. Opaque became a
painter of skies. Skies combined to become different skies.
Celestial combinations were rumoured through underground human dialogues but they would unlock no earthly
vault. Vaults opened themselves to reveal skin. Skin

animal that came to the place where they
stand now and returned to the woods
hours ago. The biggest blank page in the
world, except for these markings, which
have no intention, being waste.

I am beginning to see every surface as
something to write on, he says. I would
love to write on all of this snow.
what would you write?
Maybe I would start with my name.
well, then we could introduce ourselves prop-
erly. ill write mine too.

They separate by a hundred yards. They
begin to trudge, snow filling their boots,
jumping from letter to letter. The man
writes

author

Hits a thin patch under the H, hears the
ice beginning to crack.

The woman glides into the surface,
writing

---

turned hard. Many hard ghosts became empty. Much
emptiness found no home. Many homes burned by nail
and door. The doorframes to many passages narrowed. The
passing travellers sang to keep warm. The songs were
anathemas against windborn contagion. Contagion

love interest

laughing as she speeds up the dancing calligraphy.
They meet below the words. They read.
I guess the introduction didn't work, he says.
i don't know about that, she replies, and they turn to walk back through the path, hidden.

They are making love in an attic over-looking some scene of human activity. She is on top of him, her hair spilling into his eyes. She stops the cradling of her hips and his hands loosen on her breasts and fall to her waist. Her eyes have left his, to the window over his head, the light meeting her face like she's watch-ing a Super 8 of a childhood winter, and he is facing away from the screen. She looks out.
What do you see?
She lists: *air, clear and grey, though turning blue on your face, perhaps to blend with your sadness. a telephone wire dropping a sheath of snow as a bird lights. tree split down its trunk from the weight. fox eyes from a hollow look-ing at me. people, and their tracks. a man leading*

became a crisis despite the singing. Conscientious singers collected buckets of aid pennies by selling flowers made of plastic. Organic flowers continued to grow although ignored. Ignorance plucked living buds to decorate coffins. Coffinmakers moved up in social standing. Bookbinders

a packhorse with a yoke balancing four pails of milk. a woman fixing the burlap wrapping of a rose bush. a child carrying a rabbit in each hand by the ears towards an abattoir a scholar closing his notebook, and vanishing through an arch.

She begins to move again, because he pushes her. He feels the head of his cock rub against a pelvic bone. He winces. She stops.

Do you see anything else?

i see a young girl making a snow angel.

Hands under her ass, her thighs around his waist. He sets her on a shelving truck in the top floor of the library stacks. He goes down to her sighs. He unzips and enters her. The truck tips back into a shelf. Her hands grab at volumes of Teresa of Avila for balance before the whole shelf beats down on their twitching bodies.

One floor above, an old man falls from his shaken ladder in the Job section, shattering his ancient hip.

The books will be out of order tomorrow. After orgasms, all language must be re-alphabetized.

Her body contained the memory of the breathing of every form. The lines he

moved down, becoming itinerant. An itinerant farmhand watched a washerwoman sing in a stable. A stable burned from the torches of retreating soldiers. Torches were thrown into rivers at daybreak. The broken days played cards with each other, each card bearing the symbol of an

runs his fingers over, printed or carved.
Invisible architecture of visible ruin.
She became everything. There is but one
word for *succour*.

He often spoke of her to himself, aloud,
alone among the forms she was. His groaning and clipping of voice, sliding to high
pitch with the spliced wind.

The water continued being water,
unaware that it was her spine, the spine
he recognized. To throw forth shells.
What contained and what he made himself
into, diving.

She catalogues his scars, presses close
his skin. Her face a shroud, containing
his territories.

There are moments of gazing upon flesh
and because it gleams it pours out its
reality like a bottomless pitcher
upturned, leaving disbelief welling
behind the eyes. Vertigo has nothing to
do with height. Falling, yes -- into the
words *There is a body before me and there-*
fore I must be present.

She rises to wash the flaking skin of cum
from her stomach. Stands naked at the
sink with a blue washcloth. He lies on his
side, cupping his balls. She lifts her
right leg and places her foot on the towel

---

age. Age faltered in its straps. Straps were used on choirboys to make them sing through tender skin. Tenderness
sang underwater. Underwater divers scavenged for lost
trinkets to hawk at markets. Markets adorned themselves
with neon. Neon seeped into groundwater and hot springs

rack, swabs her hair and inside. She
leans forward, stretching. Urinates. He
listens to the ceramic trickle, many bodies emptying, many rivers receiving.

She walks home at four in the morning.
Underwear near frozen with the wet.

She begins to menstruate late one night,
and has nothing to catch the flow. She
describes the feeling of desiccation within her. *it's like leaves,* she says. She sleeps
with her hands cupping her womb, waking
up with moans and her spine curling,
reaching around to remove the lump of
bloodsoaked toilet paper, asking him to
bring more.

He catches a glimpse of his face in the
bathroom mirror as he unrolls the paper.
His complexion is sepia.

They fuck in the confessional of a cathedral. She's on the kneeler, fingernails
lodged in the wood mouldings, her skirt
lifted. He is behind her, fingers twining
her hem. He cums, silver through his
spine, his face lurching forward. He
gashes his chin open on the iron screen
through which penance will be given. He
bleeds on her neck, panting while his
cock slides out and the drops of his dissolved body fall.

---

glowed visible from space. Space closed. Closure opened
itself with new quotation marks. One set of quotation
marks looked for its twin in order to join forces and kill
the speaker. The human twins of angels who died in childbirth wondered what bright shadows lurked in mirrors.

She bolts upright with a gasp,
pulling the covers away from him.
What is it? he asks through sleep.
She points at the window and says
do you see that harp in the wall?

The world bends down. He thinks *What do
we do after the cadence?* Meanwhile, outside, there is no outside.

Suture of the chrysalis splitting from
his navel to the sheet between his knees,
and here come the crows with open and
silent beaks.

He watched her face during her orgasm
like a scientist watching the ecstasy of
pierced animals under glass. She turned
to water, having no reason to remain in
the realm of vertical balances. A flash of
colour on her cheek like the footprint of
a water ghost.
  Once he had seen a body decompose in a
time-lapse film. The eyes gave away as the
gaze turned inwards, the body anxious to
observe itself. He saw now that she was
eaten from the inside in the same way the
corpse had imploded from death reaching
out past its skin to grab at the air, to
breathe.
  Her face opened like a locket to reveal

Shadows nested in the folding air. Folds of sheep charged
over cliffs to make beautiful screaming white rainbows.
The madness of rainbows subdued itself by gazing into
calm prisms of ozone. Ozone came softly crashing down.
Down was not down but fading. Fading was language leav-

the true relics of her face. Perhaps a picture of herself taken in summer, minus
the background, minus the shadow, minus
the subtle distortions of her eyes, minus
the paper on which the photograph would
be printed.

He has seen such photochemicals in
rivers, in lakes.

Her shoulder indistinguishable from her
breast in the night. He would draw milk
in his mind, from every surface.

He falls asleep with his hand running
braille patterns over her vertebrae. Her
skin is a fabric woven by thumbless
hands. He is reading this sentence over
and over again as he falls into sleep,
trying to make sense of the string of
words. He is reading this sentence over
and over again as he falls into sleep,
trying to make sense of the string of
words. Something like shells are left on
something like a beach.

He will write this moment, and read its
sentences over and over again, falling
into sleep with editing, black lines over
blue ones, shadows over flesh. His eyes
will close on the paper, and on her flesh.

He will write this moment, using the
future tense even as he writes it now, as
though it isn't happening presently. He

---

ing isolated letters. Letters written in isolation were lost in
the post. Postings were read in smoky afternoons by unem-
ployed actors. Actors became lawyers when the theatres
were bombed. Bombs rested in the sea unexploded and
attracting shellfish. Shellfish were gathered from oil slicks

will never be sure that anything happens.
His epistemology is an embryo disassem-
bling itself in the pale effort to say the
word human.

   In other moments he thinks Let the
libraries burn. He will sleep through it
all, his limbs curling like scorched hair.

She brushes her hair as though using a
wing. Slowly, with the crook falling
against her back, her plumes folding to
close the light on this and every memory.

He had a dream he was praying a rosary,
and every bead was a burgundy grape
splitting with fermentation against his
fingertips. The dream would have had perfect meaning if he had awoken with his
fingers in her vagina. He awoke alone.
His robe draped over the chair like a
watery ghost.

Her hands were the hands he thought of
when he thought of hands. He would often
see them emerging from his own arms,
stretching towards the keyboard, his
elbows resting on the unvarnished pine.
Every key was a nipple and with these
keys he would type the word n-i-p-p-l-e.

---

at low tide and steamed over the open fires of the poor.
The poor became icons of unwritten histories. History said
I will remain unwritten so the world may continue outside
of books. Books discussed various epistemological ailments
among themselves in abandoned libraries. Libraries
became hospitals with dwindling blood supplies. Blood

Things follow on thoughts of the body.
Her words were the words he thought of
when he thought of words.

He dreamt that she spoke by pulling
unopened flowers from her mouth and
placing them in a line on an oak table. He
could not read this sentence, for it was
winter and the buds seized themselves
against him. One of the words was the
word fuck. The word fuck was a flower
where it had been a mace, wielded in neon
spangled caverns.

Meanwhile she dreamt she was chased by
a man with a knife. She cloned herself
repeatedly with hand gestures in search-
lights and left these images for the
dream-devil to rape and carve.

They awoke at the same time. He spoke of
the word fuck as a flower. She said *he
touched me here* pointing to her womb.

She leans up on her elbow and begins to
catalogue his body with a soft voice, like
a nurse listing amputations.
*your heel the arch of your foot your calf your
knee your elbow your inner arm your shin your
collarbone your chin your jaw your lips your
tongue your brow your nape your windpipe your*

---

flowed over Niagara Falls and the brokenhearted bought
postcards. The world received postcards with observations
made in short sentences. The observer craved simplicity.
Simplicity offered a stone saying This is my body. The
observer ate the stone and died of a miraculous seizure in
the twisting sentence of its intestine. Sentences were fur-

*penis. your balls. your sacrum. your intestines.
your bowels. your spleen. your scar. your voice.
your asshole.*

He is astounded at being read. Wants to
say *Gather my fragments for only you can
hold me*, but his voice too has been named,
and in naming, paralysed, and in paralysis, unable to slip down to escape the
blanket of his mind, to gather the words
that lie scattered on the floor of his dis-
memberment. She is the surgeon of undoing.
She lays down her invisible instruments
to leave invisible stains on the sheets.
She slowly pulls the mask of blue light
down from over her mouth, so to breathe
more directly the night she falls into.

He stares at the ceiling, looking for the
lined shadow on the plaster to solidify
into a thread that will stitch him. And
he knows that when his entire body heals
into a scar, nerve endings cauterized by
this monstrous love, he will be numb, and
he will depend on faith if he will ever
feel the wind pass over him again. Paces
the open window, saying *I believe the
wind is passing over me, I believe the
wind is passing over, I believe the wind
is passing, I believe the wind, I believe,
I believe that I am disappearing, I
believe that I is disappearing, I no*

---

ther shortened. Shortened to balance long silences.
Silence offered itself as a gift, though it appeared to many
to be a noose. The Boy put the noose around his neck and
listened for the change in his voice. Voices rose from beds
to close the shutters and many silent lovers suffocated.
After suffocating, the Boy fell in love. Love put its fingers

longer believe in I, believe, believe, believe.

She reaches into herself, fingers emerging with pomegranate seeds. Some she eats, some she places on his pillow, some she lets fall from the window. He wakes up. He thinks, *Being human means not wanting to be human.*

April is coming. They walk through it, gaping and filled with the smoke of winter. They both wrestle to unravel neutrality. Two blank faces saying *What unites us is a third blank face.*

There are no rules in this mystery. He decides that he will try to never write about God again.

---

around his neck. His neck blossomed with bruises. Blossoms clung to the obtusely faithful. Faith was a trap door falling away. Away was a way of falling through stages. Falling made the stage of the world disappear. Disappearance became the focus of vision. Vision created God. God sneered, saying, I've seen better, Boy.

71.

Veronica, when we were children we picked the lock on the tabernacle in the side chapel with a paper clip and stole the hosts set aside for the sick. We stuffed them into a plastic bag and went outside and fed them to pigeons caterwauling filthy through the starving afternoon cooing and arcing singlewinged against curdled sky and hammered vault to prey upon the flying crumbs of our furta sacra and with muscular breasts thunking downwards like shot meat from ice-sheathed rafters like the valleyward sackclothed penitents of any age or possible story heard to be spoken prayerfully under the light of a God who commandeers the blood of unborn martyrs for the illuminated inscription of their own future unpublished hagiographies written in the prismatic language of illegible prophecies that spin a forlorn colourwheel hubcap stolen for a trashyard altar upon which by howling petition is offered the sepulchral confession decanted into the numbered and labeled and measured and calendared reliquaries memorializing a life that would continue through its dirty verbal simulation blossoming from minds from bodies from history books from streams and rivers from urban fatigue from compromised theologies from fire escapes where the bodies that didn't make it out in time perch randomwise and blackened and mouthless gaping and dear friend these paschal victims have entered in dignified and reeking state at the end of this eucharistic meditation to say we have come, every one of us, into this world for no other reason ordained or improvised than to swallow ourselves whole.

I have returned to our old house beside the cathedral where it festers in consecrated earth. I have pried loose the plywood from the window to enter the rooms where we lived our secret marriage. No one lives here now. No one moved in after the absurd deaths of our parents. Their professions were discontinued. The Bishop can't afford as many quiet slaves anymore. He can't afford to demolish this house, either, for which I'm grateful, for I only live for my ruins. I have been here since leaving the café last night drunk. There was a scrap of blanket in our old room and I wrapped it around me and bound the finger I gashed in entering.

I will not retell any memories here. The furniture remains in its perfect arrangement. A low table. A cup by the sink. The water was disconnected. — Some rooms have been pillaged by thieves and are now strangely unroomlike in their empty state. A liquid sun is harped by the windowslats and motes of dust rise to dance in its liquor. — I had been sleeping like a slumped icon when the sun came up. I felt the light burn through my eyelids and I thought What need have I to open my eyes? — Later, the windowsill crumbled under my slow touch; paint chips fell to my feet like eczema. — Veronica, the house I would build for us would be all window and no wall. — I shat on a pile of dogshit in the corner of the old dining room while the day continued to open. I wiped my ass on a pamphlet describing birth control techniques permissible to Catholics, which had been rotting among the fallen underboards of the china cabinet. My boots crunched the shards of dinner plates eaten off of and then smashed by squatters. Shreds of mom's wedding dress over there in the corner. I will stay here all day and tomorrow as well and then I will have to leave because I will be hungry. — There will always be my longing. Hours of hunger brought on by gazing at the overflowing table. I will always be a catachumen of times and places and people and things that made me but that I did not make. Toronto. Twelfth century. Hanlan's Point. Snow. Thomas Merton. The English language. Wastes. Ironwork. Alcohol. Vermont. Wars. Fruit stands. Mirrors. Montreal, the cross on the hill. Newsboys. Vines on stonework. The word grace. Cigarettes. Nina Simone. Film, especially disintegrating inflammable gelatin. Virginity. Acquiesence. Religious medals. Geomorphic footprints. Anger. Iconography.

Fossils. Humility. The abundance of all unfinished litanies.
— I estimate that in eleven years of sad sexual awareness I
have spunked over three thousand loads of jit through my
clenched hand onto the wood and lino and dirt of this
planet and I have called your name every time. — Stay
where you are, Veronica. No. Come back. Leave. Don't
leave. Subside. Walk beside. Abide. Deride. Breathe quietly in your invisible corner. Veronica, you are sempiternal.
Make no sound to betray your absence.

Veronica, I've had this dream.

I sit with you, mother and father in a clapboard church.
Very rural. The hair of the men shines with brilliantine.
The candlelight gives a strange weight to the air. There is
a piece of twisted iron serving as a podium. The air is
methodist. This is odd because I know that we are catholic
and that the Master of this dream is a sadie-max agnostic.
The congregation is faintly lit, their faces emerging like
the bellies of fish turned up to the moon. Mother is wearing wool. Father is wearing sheepskin. You are wearing a
red velvet dress on your nine-year-old body. The ritual,
which thus far has consisted of grave voices spilling forth
inscrutable auditory shadows, pauses. The minister rises to
announce a song. Then you, Veronica, rise and approach
the slatboard stage. A thumbless old man with a patchy
scalp begins to play a chipped and wobbly concertina.

You begin to sing with a voice of fine bone. There is a
slowness in the way the words leave you, such that they
become visible in the air, as though your body was
enwrapped by a timeless arctic bent on recording your
breathing. The words become vessels. Actual vessels in the
air. Ceramics of nouns. Dishes and plates and chalices
painted with the words you sing. They hang on invisible
display hooks.

Then there is gunfire outside and the howling of oaths.
The oak doors of the church crumple like onionskin under
the shoulders of hulking woodsmen carrying muskets and
bowie knives tucked into belts of uncured hide. They smell

of creosote and saltpetre. They exhale liquor. I now understand that we are in an early Canadian colony and it's not
brilliantine in our dark hair but pig grease. They begin to
shoot. Your song continues although your accompanist has
stopped playing and scuttles under the instrument as its
keys explode by musket shot into a woodsplinter alphabet.
Your dress goes dark with urine at the thighs. The woodsmen tell you to keep singing. You continue to sing. They
begin to shoot the hanging pottery of your words, gunblack
on their faces through the haze of sulphur, magnesium and
cordite. You continue to sing. Then they take you up and
begin to inflict unmentionable acts upon your body. I
should mention now that I play no part in this dream
except to watch, for I am the pornographer of my paralysis.
The congregation fluctuates between feigned shock and
boredom, as though they were listening to a sermon. The
men rip your dress from you with their yellow teeth. They
rub hot acidic gun muzzles between the bare lips of your
vagina. One retrieves the aspergillum from its boat of holy
water and buggers you with it. Someone says Oooooh.
Another says Ahhhh. A young man grips and pumps his
cock. The minister draws nailclippers from his waistcoat
and begins his manicure. An elderly woman breaks into an
hysterical wail and her middle-aged daughter shoves a
candy in her mouth to shut her up and then readjusts her
mink stole. The old lady sucks happily with receding sobs.
The accompanist crawls out from under his exploded
instrument and takes an accordion from a leather bag and
commences to practise hymns with a circus music hobble.
The last woodsman to mount you grunts and pulls out and
shoots cum over your ass and then, drawing a fishknife
from his boot, he seizes your hip and spins you to sneer at
your sex and lifts his jagged hand to begin a crude circum-
cision. You cry out and fall limp. I will not describe your
blood, Veronica, except to say that you continued to sing.

Veronica, I don't think this dream will surprise you.

In the picture the Holy Ghost is represented by a dove. It was in that form that the Holy Ghost showed Himself visibly when St. John baptized Jesus. The dove symbolizes gentleness and peace.

The Holy Ghost dispenses the graces of God. However, the Holy Ghost produces nothing be- yond what Jesus Christ merit[...] Lord are infinite, for He i[...] merely perfects the wor[...] what similar way, the [...] nat sow new seed, i[...] been sown, making it [...]

73.

Veronica, what began as a paper cut has produced rivers of the thinnest blood on account of my haemophilia. straight to your sucking ocean.   i sail on broken bark.
no Rasputin will save me. call off the hounds of medicine; their jaws are much too bright.   my pharmacon is a gentle hysteria. i plead.   the icons shrug their square shoulders.   the birds trill outside in the dark. no let-ters will alliterate their song, and this is their glory. i hear them cast wishes towards the walls like nurses flinging milk at burial cloths. they wish for better resonance.
                    i want to say the word innocent.   i think there are two birds out there. if they were captured and put in the same cage and denied food, they would peck each other to death, starting with the eyes like two mystics in a library. in the end only one will remain singing. the survivor will be beholden by laws of retribu-tion to sing twice as much as before. as I will try to remem-ber your words, sister, as you wrote them in the airy spaces between our cage bars.   yes yes   the features of the holy face emerge in the chemical bath.
acheropita: made without hands. o you who are made without hands, please accompany me on your keyless organ.   let the scream of one birdcall about to collide with another be gathered in my palm. scuttlings in the floor.   toe. sole. heel. ball of foot. foot ball pivot feint kneecap crotch bang diddle diddle dumpling: these are thoughts, vagabonds of methodology.   i will take the humble tongue depressor as my guide. the tongue depressor is used both to open mouths for clear viewing, and to manipulate shit samples.

For once and for all I'll hunt you down and make you confess who you were to me. I'll be the aggressor this time.
— I've been doing some research. I've been prying into the secrets of your namesake like a pederast walking

through Herod's fields after the massacre of the Holy Innocents. O pray for me. O pray for me for now we that fall open like geodes mistaken for the cocoons of a new invading species of biped. We fall to the quick. We find the heart after all this poking with metal objects. The Truth has bent over with its pants down and is looking over its shoulder in a sadly coquettish way. We now come to the blank page at the centre of the world.　　　— We now find ourselves at the library looking at the subject index under your name, waiting for Meister Eckhart to light a match under our ass.　　　— There is a nun working the circulation desk. On Saturdays she helps at the blood donor clinic held in the lobby.　— Beside me there is a young woman with greasy hair and a frumpy dress bunching at the waist. She is turning the pages of Webster's Dictionary slowly. She fingers the entries. From time to time she pauses over a word and laughs a silent hysterical laugh. Actually, it's not silent. There is a slight wheeze to it. She writes the sources of her amusement in a red notebook with a knitting needle. She is in the "V" section. She says *vacancy... vaccenic acid.. vaccination ... vacillation.. ha ha ha wheeze wheeeeeeze.* — I riffle the index cards. I am discovering the academic world. I am discovering that there are those who play poker with meaning for a living. Look here. This card mentions your name in some oblique way. Queen of hearts. Lay it on the table.　— Notice how the ear canal and the vulva can be easily mistaken for each other in the mind of the naughty boy. — Jack of spades. Messenger. I sit at an oak desk and my thought-humming is like a buzz saw slicing the hemispheres of my lonely ignorance. A stacks assistant brings me dusty volumes without a word. I separate the covers like the last forensic scientist who believes in sterile conditions. Veronica, where are you? The dictionary lady is laughing: *vacuist - one who maintains that there are vacuums in nature; as opposed to a plenist... o hoohoo hoo wheeze shnarfle wheeeeeeze.*

Veronica, are you holding the cloth in the holy picture my aging teachers have left me? What is its particular weave? Are there hidden stitches? Was it made with a single thread? Do you stand before Jesus in this staged calvary I imagine for you? Do spears bristle a halo around your head? Is your face still running in negative on a printing press roller? Let me add more red. — There is a grand ker-fuffle over who you are named for. You appear codified in the Sixth Station of the Stations of the Cross, which was formalized by the Franciscans in the eighteenth century. Because of them, you are depicted in friezes. You are plas-tered and painted blue, you are cut into marble, carved into oak, you tremble in pressed tin in our scrapyard cathe-dral. The pressed tin goes bong in the cold. ... *vadimo-nium - a bond to appear before a judge on a cer-tain day... teehee.* But Veronica, I crave originals. In search of the Sixth Station, I teleport now to the Via Dolorosa. It is midday in Jerusalem. The dogs pant. The dervishes sit in dark corners mending their skirts. Barefoot children play with dreidls in the dust. Flies swarm over legs of lamb and blocks of halvah. The St. Veronica Gift Shop is doing brisk business in postcards and black velvet repros of the last supper. I see that someone has barfed on the alleged spot of the Sixth Station. Some lentils are dis-cernible in the slime, which is run over now by the cart of a Hasidic tinker who pauses to smile for a Texan's polaroid. Sigh. Nothing more to see here. Shrug. I'll beam back to the library. —The dictionary lady runs a thin hand through her scraggly hair. Her knitting needle scratches on the blank paper. Her sweater is looking good or maybe it's a balaclava. *- vagabondia, vaginate, vain-glory, vaisheshika - an orthodox philosophical system in hinduism distinguished by its atomic theory of cosmology and its belief in eternal sub-stances.. oho ho ho... - interruptions,* you used to say, dear sister, *we live for interruptions. the only true thought is the one that is interrupted by the* *present tense. the world was made to interrupt your stuttering dream of history.* — The air smells like Thomas Merton's outhouse. — Books! Bring more books! Now, the Sixth Station owes its inception to your imprinted veil, dear sister, which is allegedly kept now in the Veronica pier of the new and improved St. Peter's Basilica as designed and fortified by Michelangelo. The pier is the furthest left as you face Cattedra Petri, or Peter's Chair, thus consolidating our apostolic lineage: Christ is at the right hand of God, Peter is at the right hand of Christ, you are at the right hand of Peter and I am on my back with you sitting on my face. Peter's actual right hand is kept in a grimy glass box in Istanbul, but let us overlook this for the time being. ... *valence, valentine* ... In front of the pier stands a statue of you carved in Sicilian marble by Francesco Mochi in the seventeenth century. I don't like the statue. You look like Artemis at a bullfight. He got you all wrong. You're eastern, yes, byzantine, yes, but classical Greek? No fuckin way. You're too organic. You have too much of a fondness for blood and too little androgyny. — Oh good. I am now reading that old Francesco went mad carving this piece. He would stop in mid chisel-stroke and turn the blade on himself. I read that he carved the image of your breast into his thigh. — No one knows the exact location of the veil within the pier guarded by this fucked-up statue, but authorities assure us that it's there, and we are Guileless Believers. We can almost be sure it is in Rome at least, from the following reports: ... *valium, valkyrie - one of the maidens of odin who hover over the field of battle choosing those to be slain, titter titter ... vallecula - a groove between the base of the tongue and the epiglottis,* the dictionary lady sticks out her tongue in self-examination, *o ha hoo giggle giggle* ... In 1191, it is recorded that the veil was shown to the one-eyed King Philippe Auguste as reward on his return from a crusade in which he slaughtered and raped lotsa pickaninnies and then had his chaplain baptize their excised hearts for the glory of God. ... *valvulotomy – the operation of enlarging a narrowed heart valve by cutting through the mitral commissures to relieve the symptoms of mitral stenosis, guffaw guffaw...* The veil was said to have restored his missing eye. He was finally able to look at himself in a mirror. He admired his curly raven locks and his natty bloodspattered armour. In 1269, Marco Polo himself reports having received the gift of an asbestos shield from Kublai Khan, intended for the preservation of the *sudarium*, i.e., your veil. Swashbuckling Marco came back to Italy with spaghetti and asbestos. O Sister! It is because of your veil that the space industry has progressed in such leaps and bounds! The boys at NASA thought, Hell, if it kept the face of Christ intact for all those years, it'll keep Neil Armstrong's nuts from poaching... — Our next entry is the Holy Year of 1300, at which your veil was exposed by the notable brigand and murderer His Holiness Boniface VIII to ressurect the tourist industry in Rome. ... *vamphorn – a megaphone used in churches during the 18th and early 19th centuries, heh heh heh...* It worked. Over two million stinking people visited the stinking city that year. Innkeepers danced in the muddy streets. Much food and drink bought. Fashion shows featuring sackcloth. Many whores employed, taking two or three monks at a time. Some pilgrims were a hundred years old, carried by their children. At the sight of Rome's distant towers they broke into joyous shouts of "Roma, Roma!" Some dropped dead from joy. The sacristans of St. Peter's raked in the loot with actual rakes. Everybody was very happy. Old Dante was there. He was so moved by the event that he made it the starting date for the Divine Comedy, which on the whole is not a funny book. He stood beside a medieval roach coach hung with candied lard balls and caramelized pig tongues and took out his notebook and wrote nel mezzo del cammin di nostra vita mi ritrovai per una selva oscura che la diritta via are smarrita. He smelled a bestseller. He smiled. The concession stands did good business. Sellers of figs and tooth extractions. For the reasonable price of a half-crown you could have the crab lice picked out of your crotch with sterile tweezers. Another half-crown paid for the roadside hygienist to yank the tapeworm out of your ass. ... *vampire, vandal, vanishing cream...* And my o my, the souvenirs! Everybody wanted a commemorative brooch to take home. A guild was formed by the craftsmen who supplied this demand. They were called the Pictores Veronicarum. Like me, they made their rent by forging your face. I imagine that they had weekly meetings at which they discussed best-selling designs and marketing techniques. They often argued about how you and your veil should look. She's a sex goddess! some cried. Madonna, no! She's chaste and pure! wailed others, banging the tavern table with silver-caked hands, knocking over tankards of ale topped with scum. Sex! Chastity! Sex! Chastity! Smut! Purity! Filth! Cleanliness! and so forth. ... *vapography – the process of obtaining a developable image by permitting a sensitive film or plate to remain in contact with a substance that gives off vapours or emanations affecting it without exposure to light...* — My hand is hurting. The circulation nun has a crick in her neck and she offers up her little pain to God. I admire this greatly. My dictionary lady loses no stamina. There are floods in 1345, a revolution in 1347, a plague in 1348, and an earthquake in 1349, all of which ripened the pilgrim imagination for the Holy Year of 1350, which again featured the exposition of your Holy Veil. They were so ripe for you, in fact, that they trampled each other on the Ponte Sant'Angelo. The bodies of men, women, children and mules squeezing themselves into the sucking Tiber. ... *variable, variable nebula – a nebula whose light is subject to fluctuation variation, variety show...* The sacristans brought your veil to the riverbank and unfurled it and many of the drowning thrashed to safety despite no previous ability to swim. I add this to the list of your miracles. — Shortly afterwards, you became a reference in *Piers Plowman*. You appeared briefly in the *Pardoner's Tale*. — You will never be a footnote in my book, dear sister. I am the footnote. Look for me at the bottom of every page, fallen. — Just as Patriotic Bridge Clubs blossomed during the McCarthy era, many devotional societies grew upon your fame. Many more copies of your image were made and sold. The sellers dreamt of xerox machines and huge profit margins. Indulgences were granted to those who venerated your veil. Romans received 3,000 fewer years in Purgatory. Travellers from the rest of Italy got 6,000 years less. Foreigners landed a lucky 12,000 years off. — Hmmm. This is not a bad idea. Veronica, I hereby decree that all who read this account of your beauty also receive indulgence. For my few close personal friends, who will be obliged by guilt and pity to read this, I grant 1,000,000 years. For my acquaintances and therapists, who are less obliged to read this, I grant 2,000,000 years. For regular book purchasers, who will have chosen this book for no good reason, I grant 4,000,000 years. *variorum* - *an edition of a publication containing variant simultaneous readings of the text therein.* But wait! Arrest this conceit! A tragedy looms! Rome is sacked in May of 1527! O city! O beggars! O sewage! O your veil, sister! On May 6, a fleeing Roman named Urbano stops in a forest beyond the city walls and writes down "The holy relics have been scattered. The Veronica was stolen. It was passed from hand to hand in all the taverns of Rome without a word of protest. My hand is bleeding as I write this." *varnish, varicbed, was deferens, vasectomy, vaseline.* Your veil disappears, sweet one, allegedly buried in the St. Peter's pier. — Time passes like a helium balloon with a clown painted on it floating over a mass grave. — There is no record of anyone seeing your veil until December 8th, 1854, the first

Feast of the Immaculate Conception, when Pius IX threw a party and laid out all the relics on the banquet table next to the pickles and crustless egg salad sandwiches. Several Dukes and Marquises and Barons and Knights and Priests were there. *vassalage, vatic – of or pertaining to prophetic writings, vatican,* much high-pitched laughter at this word, *vaticide – the murdering of a prophet...* Abbé Barbier de Montault was there. He saw your veil and was the only one brave enough for the truth. He wrote that "...one cannot see the face behind, hidden by a useless metal cover, and the place of the impression exhibits only a dark surface, giving no semblance of a human face." Strangely prophetic of German Jesuit art scholar, Monsignor Josef von Filperkommen, who in 1907 saw only "a square piece of light-coloured material, somewhat faded through age, which bore two faint rust-brown stains, connected one to the other." The good Monsignor was later secretly employed as Hitler's personal art critic, targeting all acquisitions for the gleaming galleries of the Reichstag *...vaudeville, v-bomb, veal...* O sister! Could it be that your veil was as blank as a K-Mart bedsheet? — I hear the Angelus bells ring outside. The nun closes her ledger and puts on her plastic rain bonnet to go out for noon mass. I think that she believes the veil is still stashed in the pier. So do I. But where does that leave me? I still want the original. I want your life. Bring me the martyrologies! *...vectorcardiography, veda, veil, velocity of light...* Where are you? O no! Infamy! Cardinal Baronius dropped your name from the Roman Calendar of Saints in 1794! That son of a bitch. Were you no longer marketable? How many other women did he demote? Did he also refuse to use terms of endearment with his mistresses? *...velvet, veneer, veneration...* — I'm forced to use unofficial sources. Popular legends. The jottings of anthropologists. Doodles in the margins of Jesuit diaries. I consult the computers.

    Searching. Searching. System
finds   twelve   matches   for
VERONICA. A thirteenth item is
nearing publication but will
strain the boundaries of this
"subject key-word" classification...

Veronica, those who take scriptural narratives seriously say you must have been a housewife. I can imagine this. *venereal, venial, venison...* You were taking out the slops to the gutters of residential Jerusalem when you heard shouts and wails and ululations from the filthy crowd surrounding the soldiers who were leading Jesus to Golgotha. Calvary! Calvary! *venograph – photograph of a vein taken after it has been injected with an opaque substance...* You rose hurriedly, stuck your head through the glassless window, looked out over the matted heads of the crowd, and saw Him. You saw Him. Oh my. Transported by the sight, beside yourself with empathy, you seized your veil and threw yourself into the street, pushing past the lines of venders, knocking over a pile of cooking fire bricks made of camel shit. There were some who were already selling souvenirs. You were ecstatically oblivious to the insults and blows from the soldiers who pushed you back. Arriving in His Presence, you wiped His Face which poured with Sweat and Blood. You withdrew the cloth and gazed with astonishment at the image imprinted there. You were like an immigrant housewife in New York circa 1957 seeing her first polaroid. I'd love to pause and share in your wonderment, dear sister, but a Roman soldier suddenly grabs you by the tit and spits in your face. He swears in low Italian. *venomous, ventriloquism, venus's ear...* You are so beatific from your vision that you are able to admire the music in his voice. He headlocks you at cock level. Another soldier lifts his armoured skirt to fart in your face. Much laughing. Putana! he cries. You sniff the fart with calm joy. The scene passes. You turn to go home while I stand in the street like a film extra, my styrofoam coffee cup chewed at the edges. — They say that Zacchaeus was your husband, the spindle-legged tax-collector who climbed the olive tree to see Jesus paste a chunk of skin back on a leper's ass with some spit. They say that you were married to Zacchaeus although I hope you had affairs. Many. Even with Romans. I hope you nuzzled in their garlicky armpits and pushed them away when you were fulfilled regardless of whether they had cum or not, for they had a tendency to soften a little with grappa. — You carried the veil home to your husband. He was baffled in an endearing way. You knelt in front of it for days on end. Poor Zacchaeus got edgy. He was in a bad way. He was woman-less. He wanted his lentil stew. He wanted a hole to spunk in. He didn't know how to boil water for his olive-root tea. He couldn't even get you to stand up. You soiled your robe in your stunned contemplation. A week passed. Ten days. Zacchaeus got hungrier. Eleven days. Zacchaeus broke down and went to the tavern. — On the third hour of the twelfth day, which was about nine o'clock on a Wednesday morning, you heard the cry of a small bird. *...veracity, verb, verbatim...* You rose crying tears of purple joy. You gathered your things: a hair broach, a weaving comb and a blanket of your own handiwork, a wedding-day bracelet, a dowry skillet, a phial of olive oil and a leather pouch of spices. You folded the imprinted veil down to napkin size, and put everything into your basket. You walked out into the white smoke of Passach. You brushed past the sleeping body of your recently returned drunken husband. He feebly called out your name. You smiled over your shoulder and assured him you would keep him in your prayers. You exhorted him to remain chaste and holy. *...verbicide – deliberate distortion or destruction of the sense of a word...* — The world was beautiful and free and open and … ✪SAVED✪. You followed an ambiguous star to Aquitania because you heard rumour of a sick king. You entered his chamber and saw him swathed in his own feces. You unfolded the veil

and the feces evaporated and that very afternoon he sat up
to eat a meal of nuts and figs and consort with his first
concubine in months. He was now a Christian. ...*verdict
verdigris, vergilian*... You left him grinning like an
obese child who has been told how he looks robust and
healthy instead of fat and ugly. — You went on to other
quarry. You had an eternal city to conquer. And, luckily,
the emperor was sick! Tiberius had an unbalanced accu-
mulation of Bilious Humours in his Achilles tendon! His
jugular coursed with Stygian Scum! The doctors of Hera
were dumbfounded. They consulted the Diagnostic
Handbook stolen from Babylon. They cast spells against
Carthaginian Succubi. They patrolled the terracotta roofs
for that tricky Spartan Chimney Goblin. They scribbled
out improvised prescriptions on their wax tablets. They
chewed their styluses nervously. — You entered Rome
with great fanfare, all the beggars singing a newly composed hymn in your honour, sporting their leprosy like
snowy victory banners. Meanwhile, Tiberius writhed in
the palace infirmary. You entered like a 16-year-old Liz
Taylor walking into a Hollywood orgy and smiling calmly.
At first he regarded you with suspicion, and ordered
another burnt offering to made to Jupiter. You asked him
to turn away from his heathen altar, which stank like a
middle-class barbecue. You unfurled the veil and said *o
leader of nations: there is but one good and this is
his face.* Tiberius stopped shivering and farting. He held
his belly in confusion. The Cerberean Bile drained from
his countenance and his three faces collapsed into one. He
thanked you and offered you more gold and gave you a
room in the palace decorated with bouquets and little
cards with red hearts on them and threw a banquet in your
honour and tried to convince you to become his sixth
wife. You refused with such grace that he was not angry.
They say you lived in Rome for the rest of your days. You
were buried in a catacomb, and your incorruptible body
was translated to the old St. Peter's in the 12th century.

The hangnail of one of the gravediggers was miraculously cured. — But now, even your tomb is gone, destroyed by Michelangelo's demolition team in 1606. The ruins of the Veronica chapel lie under the tiles that support the Pieta this very day, which is a day of shitty weather. *...veridical hallucination - a hallucination corresponding to a real event, as when the apparition of an image of an absent person is coincident with her death...* Incidentally, it is my supposition that the frustrated sculptor who recently fell on this same Pieta with a hammer and hacked off the Virgin's milky nose was mimicking that renaissance wrecking crew. I know why he did it. I, too, have been terrorized by beauty. Forgive me, but I would have gone for the bosoms. Likewise, the woman in me zeroes in on David's immaculate dick. What an exquisite art iconoclasm is! Was no one interested in the precise arc of his angry hammer swing? Did the police pause to admire the random placement of a marble chip before drawing a crude chalk circle around it? Why was our hammer man not allowed to stand beside his creation and smile for the paparazzi? — We are now in old St. Peter's to look at your old tomb. In through the Guidonea *...verifiability principle - a proposal of early logical positivists according to which a requirement or criterion for the meaningfulness of a factual statement is its susceptibility to the possibility of being either theoretically or actually proven true or false by reference to empirical facts...* — Look up and see the rotted inscription. We read "Berenice." Is this a misspelling? A derivation from an earlier time? — Veronica, I now learn that you are associated with Berenice, the woman famous to the Byzantine rite as the woman with the hemorrhage of twelve years. The one who touched His cloak and was healed. I want a connection here. Were you the holy bleeder? Was the image of the face on your veil a politically motivated misprision of you holding forth your menstrual rag to the Son of God?

Was this an ancient Hebrew act of seduction? *verisimilitude - the appearance of truth.* Your funeral slab is oval, the form of deliverance, Ova, Ovarian cyst, Open, a slab of purple and white porphyry on which your body was said to have been laid out in death. This is where your incorruption began. This is where the demolition men sniffed you and went mad, swinging axes. Beside you is red Egyptian-stone sarcophagus in which Hadrian IV was laid in his finest pope hat and slippers in the 12th century. — Aha! Things are beginning to make sense to me. Old Hadrian was an Englishman. The scholars fail to speculate on this connection. I hereby propose that this is how you learned our fine English language, dear sister. You were tutored out of your lower-class Aramaic by a dead pope from Hertfordshire! *verjuice - the sour juice of crab apples or unripe grapes.* He whispered declensions into the damp air. You repeated them like a schoolgirl lapping ice cream. *i haff died you haff died he hass died she hass died we haff died dey haff died; i die you die he dise she dise we die dey die; i weel die you weel die he weel die she weel die we weel die dey weel die; dat wan ees eeee-see meeeester chhhhadrian.* This is how you learned the tongue with which you haunt me now! Hadrian was our meal-ticket to world-wide colonial dissemination! — But, wait! Where is your body, dearest? To what hidden place did they translate you after 1606? *vermiculation - penetration by worms: the state of being worm-eaten.* — Holiness is near. It smells of pine forests. What makes this hour holy? What has been compressed, or deleted? The memory stops, the story is given over to undifferentiation. Who would perpetrate such myths as the holy hour condemns? Who has stopped on the stairwell, and is looking at old family pictures, and crying? Who has given up on a screenplay after describing the opening pan of the sky? Who has forgotten their sex and collapsed their years? Who has stopped kicking in the womb? I have no answers. Who has put down their rifle or scythe because of a strange sound or movement in the brush? Who has stopped addressing an invisible friend? Who has stopped demanding response from Nothing? Who has stopped keeping track of the books they have lent out? The circulation nun has returned. I hope her mass was a beautiful and enriching experience. Who has stopped inscribing? The dictionary lady is persistent. Who knows what holy is? Who has decoded the Accident? *vermilinguia – a division of lizards consisting of the chameleons...* — Here it is. The last reference to your name, in *Speculum Ecclesiae* of Gerald of Wales, 1199. He visited Rome to ask the pope if he could be made into a bishop. I like his honesty. He said "Um, er, excuse me, Mr. Pope, ummm, can I please be a bishop if I give you lots of money please, please, please?" He was also intrigued by your story, sister. He played detective to your name, and wrote the following sentence, which is both my truest knowlege and my complete undoing: **"And some maintain, playing upon the name, that Veronica is so called from "vera iconia", that is to say, 'true image'."** Here we have it. *...vermilion...* I am finished. The truth I sought is now complete because it is now hidden forever. Who would have known it would take so long? Is that all your name is, sister? Has this all been a game? Are you but a legend, dear sister? *...verminosis – infestation with or disease caused by parasitic worms...* A pedagogical construct? A cloud of absent wishes pulling me around on a leash? Were you made up for my benefit? Do you make Calvary more human, more palatable, easier for the screenplay writers? Where are you? Is your life subordinate to your relic? Trumpets. *...vermont snakeroot – a form of wild ginger...* Clarions. I ride the wave of half light. I have come to the last knowlege: **YOUR STORY, DEAR SISTER, YES, INDEED, YOUR LIFE, WAS MADE UP TO SUBSTANTIATE A RELIC.** This is what literature is, sweet Veronica. This is what life is, sister. A vast and intricate dream of evidence for the dead things we find inhabiting our souls. I did not want to know this. — And which relic do we speak of here? Me. I am the relic. I am so tired. — Is it an unforgivable cliché to cry out that I have come to the end of my language for finding you? *vernacular - a language that is spoken or written naturally at a given period.* But I will do so anyway, in defiance of the next ugly truth, which is that these findings do not mean that my world will end. I will close up these books when they ring the closing bell here in the library, I will leave, sit on the step of the old cathedral, have a cigarette, be mildly annoyed at the foul taste it leaves. I will go home, eat canned food, and listen to my record of Nina Simone while looking out of a grimy window. This evening will be like any other. Nothing will change. Knowlege rarely manifests itself in the body of the knower. In the same way, there is no difference in the appearance of an empty chalice and the chalice that is filled with Blood in the eyes of the one who kneels before it. This kneeler could only know the difference if there was a mirror suspended over the vessel. But tests have proven that there is nothing in the sky upon which we may hang such mirrors. Skygazers like us, Veronica, never see ourselves in bright definition. *vernal - appearing or occurring in the spring.* long pause, long pause, long pause *...veronica...*, and for the last time, there is much laughter. And the ringing of bells.

74.

"Roused in fury against the altars that have been able to snatch from us some few grains of incense, our pride and our libertinage shatter them as soon as the illusion has satisfied our senses, and contempt almost always followed by hatred instantly assumes the pre-eminence hitherto occupied by our imagination." — de Sade, ibid.

Once I saw something very beautiful. A swallow flew in through a clerestory window. It saw the dove of the Holy Spirit painted at the apex of the dome over the main altar. It wanted to mate with the image. It fluttered against the plaster, trying to land on the painted perch, trying to grasp the painted olive branch. In its confusion, its desire increased. A madness came over it. The swallow struck the plaster with fury. It began to injure itself and the fresco. Chips of stucco came away, creating jagged edges upon which the swallow lacerated its cheek and breast. Soon both the image and the bird were mangled and smeared with blood.

There are those who float through the world. They regard the drowning with confusion. The drowning are often embarrassed in their thrashing. The drowning compensate by trying to make their drowning look good.

I've just read my first newspaper in a year. On page four I am sure I located a perfect action in this universe. In Merrion, Kansas, a 26-year-old man cut his right eyeball from its socket and flushed it down the toilet. He explained later to the reporter leaning over his hospital bed that it had contained a satanic symbol. The reporter used the medical clipboard from the foot of the bed to support his notebook. His pencil scratched and he cracked his gum. The night shift boys at Reuters sat up in their Manhattan offices and translated the story into 54 languages. They made jokes about it over hot and sour soup in a 24-hour Chinese restaurant. The following morning, the story appeared in the margins of 258 newspapers worldwide.

The toilet bit takes the cake. "Fuckin eye," he must have

thought, blood dripping from his chin. "It's evil as shit. I should put it in the toilet. [**Flush.**] There it goes." I love this guy. He knows that there is no romance in the perfect action. Flesh is not a trophy. Wounds are not souvenirs. I declare this to be a Perfect Action.

Because of this story, I now suspect that Perfect Actions are happening everywhere, at all times, in drive-thrus and honky-tonks, in truck-stops and sheds behind clapboard churches in razed corn fields. Perfect Actions sometimes leak word to the reporters. The reporters are sometimes awake and listening.

I want to start dreaming Perfect Actions... a cherry branch falls on a pram and the pram is empty... a child totters on a balcony and the wind returns her balance... something reminds somebody of something else.

Today I went outside and sat on a crate to watch things, and research Perfect Actions. This is what I saw. An apple on a fruitstand table is handled by a black girl holding a mulatto baby, a mechanic with grease over his brow, a beggar with a starving dog, a prostitute on his way to business college, a surgeon after a nine-hour double bypass, a 42-year-old pregnant Catholic woman and three other children clinging to her skirts, a secretary with a gold-buttoned dress. I sit on my crate with my attention focused like a sleepy boy with a toy gun targeting a dove.

The apple soon grows dull with disinterested fingers. The sun browns its meat. It is packed and unpacked from a cracked wooden crate with red Farsi script. If it is winter it is moved by hands in fingerless gloves and it is moved many more times, as the cold slows decay. It is held midair while the handler is distracted by shouts from the street. By night a parasite enters. It lays eggs, all pearly and wet. The brown flesh goes soft with movement. This is a Perfect Event, coinciding with Perfect Actions. (Do I add to Perfection by writing about this ?Ask the r e a d e r. She knows.) When dripping with fermentation and worm castings, the apple is discarded from hand to hand like a primitive mythology in a cocky graduate seminar for literary theory. It nestles into styrofoam in the city dump where seagulls scream at crows as they dive and are buffeted by waves of rising gas. We are reminded of the beauty of mass graves.

Where are you? Hand me your 's all your bitter Eden 's. I can be faithful. I promise to bleed to death by licking the blood on the blade of the leg trap in the forest. I am grateful for spices. I promise to abide by my words long after speaking them. I promise to require little light for my work so as to develop eyes for the night. I promise to count the lines in the woodgrain of my table. I promise to honour all material things that did not choose to surround me. I will sell myself for the future anterior. I promise to sing myself hoarse while I walk myself into starvation. I promise to never ask whether I have been heard. I promise to fast from my diet of dreams and offer my empty mind to those overtaken by thought. I am grateful for these hands which translate my gratitude for hands by moving through pad and finger over these keys to find the letters that spell the word h-a-n-d-s and then reach for the delete button to correct my grateful sentence when my hands become clumsy with ecstasy. I am grateful for the plastic star in this creche beside my typewriter. I promise the star I will paint it gold. I am grateful for its beams that I imagine. I promise my imagination the power to hold me forth. I promise to be grateful for this star that is not real but is essential as the Cryer of Plastic Unbelievable Faith.

I play a lot of pinball now. There's a Playboy pinball machine down at the Portuguese pool hall. There are cartoon bunny-girls painted on the bumpers. Their voice-bubbles say things like "Ya gotta have STEEL BALLS to play PINBALL." One row of targets is cartoon breasts. Another row is cartoon asses. The Portuguese guys still don't know who I am, though I'm there every day, recapturing the mechanical, the peace of geometry singing in the glass box… the information all honestly visible… the game you can understand…

After our houses burn, after our churches and parlia-
ments and supreme courts have been firebombed, we sit on
the charred furniture in our white clothes, speaking in
whispers among fluttering embers of curtains. When we
whisper it is with the throats of stillbirths, our vowels
engaged to the suckling reflex. And what do we whisper?
We whisper apologies. We recant. We repent. We are our
own tender inquisitors. We whisper so as not to hear the
words we speak, for they are ineffectual. We whisper when
unable to avail ourselves of the sacrament of silence,
which is all we want, from our deepest memories of earth
to our most colourless dreams of ascension.

Imagine the voices of a book as strands of fishing wire.
Assume that each strand is of the same length. Half are
laid in parallel lines one half-inch apart. The other half
are laid on the perpendicular to these, also one half-inch
apart. Let us call these halves syntax and tense, or space
and time. The resulting intersections are then knotted
together by the fisherman, and the ends of the grid are
fixed to a metal hoop or a thick coil of rope.

The fisherman casts the net.

There is always the possibility that a fish much too large
for the size and weight of netting will cause these strands
to tangle horribly. In contemporary times, fishing wire
(i.e., space and time) is mass-produced on such a scale by
so many multinational companies that the fisherman is
encouraged to abandon the net (tangled around the body,
let us imagine, of a dolphin), purchase more wire, and simply string another. Let us say, however, that this story hails
from a more antiquated time, and the tangled wire represented the worth of an entire year's catch. We can be sure
that the ancient fisherman will unbind the dolphin, give
its cold blue corpse a decent water burial, and spend days
untwining the strands with numb and shaking fingers. He
trembles because the process ages him.

See how he sits on his stool, the embers of a driftwood
fire in his stone hearth, his hands memorizing the tangles

for the day on which he goes blind. Notice how the oil lamp in the corner flickers as it conducts the sea currents from beyond his door. See how its light throws itself upwards onto his tear-streaked face. See how he looks like he is reading the book that tangled itself when it snagged the unspoken dolphins of his memory.

Today is March 25th, 1995. Today is the feast of the Annunciation. I have a quarter to my name and I'm dreaming of payphones. — All I want from this life, sister, is to step into a phone booth, spend my last quarter, and dial a number. All I want is to say "Hi. It's me." — I've often thought about what fun it would be to take one of those cellular phones, grease it down with vaseline, and then stick it up my butt. Then I'd walk to a row of payphones in the McDonald's downtown and dial the number for the cellular phone and see how long it would take before people couldn't help but to look up from their shitburgers to stare at my ringing ass.

I blame* all things verdant with erosion. I blame the facts. I blame my desire for apocalypse, fed by reruns of the A-Team. I blame all economies of material employment. I blame mass-market mysticism. I blame all Catholic educators for being intellectual abortionists. I blame the Thorny Path. I blame continental drift. I blame geologists investing in dynamite companies. I blame marching bands for the general inanity of public celebrations. I blame the satellite dish. I blame the white coat. I blame the black robe. I blame architects in their blue houses. I blame the fluorescent lights of pharmacies. I blame children for making me soft with gratitude. I blame the Christian Brothers not for desiring little boys but for not writing love poems to them. I blame the modernists for sweetening my myths through Euclidean distilleries. I blame the choirmaster for conducting out of anything but anger. I blame sexual differentiation. I blame the Accuser, who has given me many

---

* "In cases of epilepsy we spit, that is, we throw back contagion at contagion." — Pliny, *Naturalis historia*.

masks. I blame the poetics of solitude, excess and non-locality. I blame the ass I sit on for being priggish about who enters it when and with what. I blame God and God dodges me by saying FUCK OFF, I'VE DONE NOTHING TO GET UPSET ABOUT, NOTHING YOUR INVOLUN-TARY BAPTISM OF SPITTLE AND PISS DIDN'T PRE-PARE YOU FOR, MY BOY, SO GET LOST AND STOP WASTING MY **TIME.** So I blame you instead, you who have made me thin by trading your hope for my vanity.

Veronica, someone has just suggested that I retitle this novel *Veal.* I just don't know what to think.

Rainy afternoon. Listening to Nina Simone sing "Blues for Mama". Here it comes, my favourite line. Her throat and my ear strung to the same metallic drum.

> *Ain't nobody perfect*
> *cause ain't nobody free,*
> *hey-yey-yey-yey, Lordy Mama-a-a,*
> *watchoo go-o-o-o-na do-oo?*

I'm remembering Mom now. I neglected to mention that Bishop _____ used to fuck her. Weekday mornings, mostly. She'd get cornered while cleaning the toilet or the bath in the rectory. How could I have left this out? Was it because Our Father didn't notice? Or did he, but was too drunk to care? Maybe I left it out because it was just too obvious, given the rest of the narrative. Anyway, for all her beauty, Mom deserves a revenge, if only in the form of a wish: do you remember, sis, how her fingertips were always embedded with splinters of glass? Well, consider this. One day Mom wakes up really early to work on the window. She does a lot of scoring. She cuts all the pieces out for a Magdalen figure. She loads up her fingertip cal-luses with glass splinters. Later, her inviting smile and deft hipshuffles make the Bishop exclaim "Well, now you're getting the idea." She unzips his black trousers (which she'd pressed the day before), and com-mences a glass splinter handjob. She talks dirty. She smiles and licks her lips. It hurts the Bishop like hell but feels too good to let her stop. His stubby dick goes raw and bloody. Later he picks out the splinters with tweezers, bawling his eyes out. Fragments of silver, gold, and turquoise, glittering in the light of his reading lamp.

Electric eels spark in the sewers under my apartment. I daydream that somewhere they sing happy songs while they gut the fish.

74.

Life is not a **dreambook.** ¡Careful! ¡Careful! ¡Careful!
— variation on a line by Lorca

Many strange things happen at the end of this story. Our hero is The Man of Random Apocalypses, known from previous Series as The Boy of Probable Beginnings. In issue #93 T(i)MRA confesses **EVERYTHING IMPORTANT** into a hand-held tape recorder. He sits on a balcony. Cloud sentences float by. He fills one side of a micro-cassette used to save telephone messages. He takes the machine to a cemetery and sets it beside a desiccated bouquet in a mausoleum at the top of a hill. He plays the tape at full volume. Then TiMRA turns and retreats through the moss-eaten stones dropping their names like forgotten currency. His body is like a ball-bearing sealed into one of those dime store plastic games in which the child tilts the surface this way and that to steer the trapped object through a maze of moulded plastic headstones, if only to have it drop into a hole at the bottom. God was absently practising His own hand-eye coordination. — TiMRA's recorded voice rolls over the stones. The dead bodies add a spongy resonance. He keeps walking. He decides he's absolved when he's so far away from the machine he can no longer hear his voice. He has no way of knowing whether the tape has ended or he's out of earshot. The sound is like that of a transistor carried away from the signal source by an escaped convict listening for the latest police reports concerning his whereabouts. The tape could be running even now, although he would never know it. It hardly matters, for even his unrecorded thoughts are now screamed away by the backhoe which has come to dig another grave, digging like a dog implanted with machine parts that make it paw involuntarily through miles and miles of sod, although it knows there are no bones to be had, but it must obey its Remote Control and lurch around and piss on itself and give everybody a good laugh.

Another issue portrays TiMRA becoming the Ghost of a Singular Destiny by weeping so much that he goes blind. Unable to see the divisions of the world anymore, which had caused him to weep, he concentrates on orchestrating the Voices into a choral speech that would sound the same anywhere in the world, day or night, played beginning to end or end to beginning. Blind, humming, writing, and weeping like an idiot, he finally has a vocation. His tears make the notes run down his paper, smearing the polyphony into a unison of black ink.* The illustrator has drawn a vaguely feminine ghost-figure in the background of the final panel. The voice-balloon of the figure contains the words: *it is perfectly natural that you can't manage to sing a last sentence of regret or praise. please remember that to say amen means 'this is agreeable to us' not 'the end'.*

---

* Respect for the dead requires that cemeteries be properly kept. We should remember that the bodies of the buried will one day rise again to join immortal souls and live forever with God.

Respect for the dead would also advise us to give up the recent fad of dolling up corpses, painting their faces to make them seem alive, as if they were prepared for some flighty show. — My *Catholic Faith*, by The Most Reverend Louis LaRavoire Morrow, D.D., Bishop of Krishnagar, Wisconsin, 1949.

75.

"The many little failures of magic are less disturbing to believers than the one big periodic failure of the millennium, and are more easily explained away."
— Bryan Wilson*

76.

(possible epilogue)

The night of cedar and balsam plies its currents. Your weeping is the implementation of a sad, genetic grammar. The cocoons sway gently in the breeze. In Toronto or New York or Sofia or Dresden, an oblivious museum attendant has left the escalator running all night, to carry an endless procession of ghosts to examine the calcified footprints and mummies they have left behind.

Behind you, veiled by an overturned funnel of mist, the cathedral catches dust on its stone petals. The scribes are tucked away in bed, dreaming of celestial libraries.

At home, the synthetic palm-trees in the lobby of your apartment building feed quietly on fluorescence. Penile implants between the thighs of impotent lawyers deflate gently in the summer night. True lovers sleep.

Here, the trees are your copyists, absorbing your image so many times that you emerge from the forest, bodiless,

---

* from *Magic and the Millenium: A Sociological Study of Religious Movements of Protest Among Tribal and Third-World Peoples* (New York, 1973). Let me not forget, however, the words of the more famous Brian Wilson, the Beach Boy. You know, the one who lay in bed for three years, depressed because, evidently, California did not save the world. He once answered my question, sister, about how I was to live my life. He crooned through my transistor

be true to your school
like you would to your girl...

invisible. You have dematerialized without asking for death. You have been redeemed without asking for redemption. You are loved because of

77.

I can still see you, Sister.

In the summer, I see you from a window, alone in a garden, one hand twined with a rosary, the other gracing fruit. Beads and berries caressed with the touch my flesh once knew. A raspberry stain on the edge of your habit from wiping your brow. Prayers said with seeds in the teeth.

In the fall, I see you sitting alone among the chaff, making a rosary out of dried cranberries, corn flax braided tightly into a cross.

Now, in the season of ripe fermata, I see you alone in the snow. Seen from the same window, I see you, sister, alone in the snow. A rosary wrapped around your left wrist, glass beads clicking like icicles.

What will you say when the words are beaten out of you, when they spill through wounds?

You turn in the snow to map your loneliness — wood shed, library, cathedral, scaffolding for the mosaic-workers, a grotto with the Queen crowned with ice and holding a frozen child, headless stalks of cut roses emerging from the stone orbit of her crescent moon pedestal. Tiny feet of white marble. You lie down to make a snow angel, the snow moulding itself to your shoulders, your spine, the backs of your legs. When rising again you lose your balance, your hand piercing the form of the chest, your fingers sinking to the unseen grass, blades sharpened by frost. You have the urge to squat and defecate in the white. The tension in your back deepens your shivering.

Veronica is alone in the snow. Nothing May Happen. If something happens, what will she say? How will she translate the breath she uses now to hum to herself? Who will listen? If a nun is raped by the Holy Spirit in a forest and there is nobody around to hear, does she make a sound? Veronica is alone in the snow.

She fantasizes of whistling at such a pitch that the convent library will shatter. She will be buried under books that do not contain her name.

78.

I wish that you could represent yourself, so that you would indeed be alone in the garden, alone in the snow, freed from the words that describe you. In my mind I want you to believe that you are alone. In my heart I want to share in your solitude while remaining invisible. I know that if you lift your head and catch my eye from the window, you would feel violated, and I would duck away. This is how the mind falls in love with its fictions. This is how the fictions learn to hate the mind that wants to possess them. This is how human attention destroys the subject it desires to shine upon.

If you indeed speak directly to me, it will be because I force myself to believe that I am you. And if I become you, I can happily abandon my body. You will speak my death. At the sound of your opening throat, I will fall from the window from which I watch you now, and you will think the rustle in the brush and the snapping of my neck are the scuttlings of some small animal through kindling. You will smile and continue to pray, comforted by the delicate movements of the world.

Other titles from Insomniac Press:

What Passes for Love
short stories by Stan Rogal
   What Passes for Love is a collection of short stories that shows the dynamics of male-female relationships. These ten short stories by Stan Rogal resonate with many aspects of the mating rituals of men and women: paranoia, obsession, voyeurism, even assimilation.
   Stan Rogal's first collection of stories, *What Passes for Love*, is an intriguing search through many relationships and the emotional turmoil within them. Stan's writing reflects his honesty and unsentimentality, previously seen in his two books of poetry and published stories. Throughout *What Passes for Love* are paintings by Kirsten Johnson.
5 1/4" x 8 1/4" • 144 pages •trade paperback with flaps
isbn 1-895837-34-0 • $14.99

Bootlegging Apples on the Road to Redemption
by Mary Elizabeth Grace
   This is Grace's first collection of poetry. It is an exploration of the collective self, about all of us trying to find peace; this is a collection of poetry about searching for the truth of one's story and how it is never heard or told, it is only experienced. It is the second story, our attempts with words to express the sounds and images of the soul. Her writing is soulful, intricate and lyrical. The book comes with a companion CD of music/poetry compositions which are included in the book.
5 1/4" x 8 1/4" • 80 pages • trade paperback with cd
isbn 1-895837-30-8 • $21.99

The Last Word
an insomniac anthology of canadian poetry
edited by michael holmes
   The Last Word is a snapshot of the next generation of Canadian poets, the poets who will be taught in schools — voices reflecting the '90s and a new type of writing sensibili-

ty. The anthology brings together 51 poets from across Canada, reaching into different regional, ethnic, sexual and social groups. This varied and volatile collection pushes the notion of an anthology to its limits, like a startling Polaroid. Proceeds from the sale of *The Last Word* will go to Frontier College, in support of literacy programs across Canada.

5 1/4" x 8 1/4" • 168 pages • trade paperback
isbn 1-895837-32-4 • $16.99

Desire High Heels Red Wine
Timothy Archer, Sky Gilbert, Sonja Mills and Margaret Webb
   Sweet, seductive, dark and illegal; this is *Desire, High Heels, Red Wine*, a collection by four gay and lesbian writers. The writing ranges from the abrasive comedy of Sonja Mills to the lyrical and insightful poetry of Margaret Webb, from the campy dialogue of Sky Gilbert to the finely crafted short stories of Timothy Archer. Their writings depict dark, abrasive places populated by bitch divas, leather-clad bodies, and an intuitive sense of sexuality and gender. The writers' works are brought together in an elaborate and striking design by three young designers.

5 1/4" x 8 1/4" • 96 pages • trade paperback
isbn 1-895837-26-X • $12.99

Beds & Shotguns
Diana Fitzgerald Bryden, Paul Howell McCafferty, Tricia Postle and Death Waits
   Beds & Shotguns is a metaphor for the extremes of love. It is also a collection by four emerging poets who write about the gamut of experiences between these opposites from romantic to obsessive, fantastic to possessive. These poems and stories capture love in its broadest meanings and are set against a dynamic, lyrical landscape.

5 1/4" x 8 1/4" • 96 pages • trade paperback
isbn 1-895837-28-6 • $13.99

Playing in the Asphalt Garden
Phlip Arima, Jill Battson, Tatiana Freire-Lizama and Stan Rogal

This book features new Canadian urban writers, who express the urban experience — not the city of buildings and streets, but as a concentration of human experience, where a rapid and voluminous exchange of ideas, messages, power and beliefs takes place.

5 3/4" x 9" • 128 pages • trade paperback
isbn 1-895837-20-0 • $14.99

Mad Angels and Amphetamines
Nik Beat, Mary Elizabeth Grace, Noah Leznoff and Matthew Remski

A collection by four emerging Canadian writers and three graphic designers. In this book, design is an integral part of the prose and poetry. Each writer collaborated with a designer so that the graphic design is an interpretation of the writer's works. Nik Beat's lyrical and unpretentious poetry; Noah Leznoff's darkly humourous prose and narrative poetic cycles; Mary Elizabeth Grace's Celtic dialogues and mystical images; and Matthew Remski's medieval symbols and surrealistic style of story; this is the mixture of styles that weave together in *Mad Angels and Amphetamines*.

6" x 9" • 96 pages • trade paperback
isbn 1-895837-14-6 • $12.95

Insomniac Press • 378 Delaware Ave. • Toronto, ON, Canada • M6H 2T8
phone: (416) 536-4308 • fax: (416) 588-4198

Respect for the dead requires that cemeteries be properly kept. We should remember that the bodies of the buried will one day rise again to join immortal souls and live forever with The Reader.

Respect for the dead would also advise us to give up the recent fad of dolling up corpses, painting their faces to make them seem alive, as if they were prepared for some flighty show or video.